softly she waits for winter

a jakub riser novel

SION JONES

softly she waits for winter

a jakub riser novel

by

SION JONES

Aethem Press - Austin

Damn you, Bernie, you got me into this.

Aethem Press - Austin

ISBN Information:
Hardcover : 978-1-956558-15-9
Paperback : 978-1-956558-14-2
E-book : 978-1-956558-16-6
Kindle: 978-1-956558-11-1

Table of Contents

a little harder

Bars never seem to attract normal people.

Like that guy with the black messenger bag. He was a bit odd. Never a beer, never a shot, and for some reason he couldn't order a normal drink to save his life. Always some cocktail knockoff, usually a Mojito of some sort, always virgin. Apparently like his dating life, because the kid never showed up with a woman and rarely talked to the ones that *were* there. Bad business for liquor sales, good for refreshing his bartending skills.

At least it would end up making him more valuable in the bartending market until he could find something better to do.

He'd taken the job at the Tinder Statesman because he was tired of trying his hand at physical jobs and just wanted a change of scenery to pay the bills and not make him want to soak in a tub of liniment every night after work. This did both, and for the most part, he was happy.

Today was slower than usual, but it was 4:30 on a Tuesday, so you only really got the regulars in the door, and this guy was usually the first in, and he was out by dinner time. Happy Hour seemed to chase him out the door every day. Yet another reason why he was so odd.

"Excuse me, Mitchell? Could I have another one of these please?" The guy asked, lightly tapping the rim of his glass. It was absolutely irritating.

"I'm *not* Mitchell, I'm Stefan," he huffed, feeling the anger rise. Then he remembered that his name tag actually did have his first name on it. He looked down, glanced at the brass shine, and softened. "Fat Man in the back," he started. "Sorry. I go by Stefan, but the boss man refuses to put anything but my legal first name on the tag, so we have this crap."

"Well, Stefan, some bosses just suck. I apologize for the mistake."

Maybe this guy wasn't *that* bad.

"No harm done, I guess."

"So how did that whole thing come about, if you don't mind me asking?"

"What thing?"

"With the name. The difference."

"Welp, my biological father named me Mitchell, and Momma wanted to name me Stefan. I was supposed to be Stefan Mitchell, but my father had all the access to the people doing the paperwork cuz momma was in the back getting stitched up or whatever and he thought her idea of a name would turn me into a gay hairdresser so I ended up Mitchell Stefan. Momma always called me Stefan.

She didn't give a shit, and I don't think she ever forgave 'im for it. Nobody uses Mitchell."

"What does your daddy call you?" The kid asked.

"He doesn't. He ran off with some waitress and moved west, from what I understand. Never saw him again. Honestly, I don't remember what he looked like. Couldn't pick 'im out of a lineup to save my life."

"I had the opposite problem."

"Oh yeah?," Stefan asked, intrigued.

"Yeah, my mom ran off with her nurse, so my dad blew his brains out."

Wow.

"You said your mom ran off with her nurse?"

"Yeah, she's a lesbian now. She's also very highly outclassed by her partner."

"I thought I had a messed up story, that's so screwed up it makes mine look normal! What's your name, anyway? You've never said."

"Jakub. With a 'u'. I come from the eastern Hill country, so we spell things weird sometimes. La Grange, actually. Jakub Riser."

Stefan took a moment to examine the sandy-haired man again. He looked on closer inspection to roughly be the same age, so he wasn't really a kid, but that didn't explain the stuffed black rabbit he carried around with him in a sling bag. At the present moment, it was perched, facing Jakub as if it were a real thing.

"I'm sure you get this a lot, but the curiosity is killin' me. What's with the rabbit?"

Jakub slightly smiled and answered, "Oh, Luna? She's a gift from one of my better loves. My last, actually."

"Hard breakup? Women can do that to ya."

"Now that you mention it, it was a hard break. She's dead."

Not the answer I was looking for.

"I'm sorry. Maybe sometimes I should just keep my damned mouth shut."

"Nah," Jakub answered with nothing but kindness on his face, "You're good. People do ask a lot. It's an odd thing, I'll admit."

"Anyway, I know where La Grange is. That ain't too far away. So, Jakub with a 'u', What's the story with you coming into a bar and never orderin' alcohol? Kinda defeats the purpose, doesn't it?"

"Not really," Jakub answered, "I figure it this way. I have the drinks that I like, and you know ya can't get a virgin mojito or many of the other drinks that I drink at the grocery store, so I think it's easier to just come here and have them naturally made by the professionals."

"You know you could just make 'em at home. It's not that hard and probably costs a lot less. Not that I don't appreciate the business."

"I like the social interaction. All I have is a fish at home, and she sucks at tending bar. Gets me out of the house and out into the real world, at least for a little bit. Used to just drink straight bourbon at home, then that wasn't working out so well for me. Better to not do it at all where I'm concerned."

"Okay. I just thought I'd run that by ya. Lemme know if there's anything else I can get ya."

He had gone back to cleaning up bar, making sure ice was in, and doing some light cleaning when he noticed something odd was happening.

The guy, Jakub, with a "u", began talking to the chair next to him.

It was empty.

They appeared to be having a lively conversation when Jakub had waved to him and asked for a gin and ginger tonic for the imaginary friend next to him. Called him Garry. It was definitely a new one.

"Garry here wants a gin and ginger. Says he keeps asking for one. Guess you just didn't hear him."

"I didn't. Might be a reason for that."

Like the fact that he's an invisible, imaginary friend of yours that has no voice?

"Okay," the kid seemed confused, almost offended.

"You're wanting a gin and ginger tonic, you said?"

"Yeah, I'll go ahead and pay for his drink, and get another of my usual. The rest is yours." The kid placed a twenty-dollar-bill on the counter.

Can't argue with that.

After all, the guy had paid for it, and why turn down the tip? If he decided someone was actually there, then might as well play along. This Jake guy might be falling off the wagon, who could tell?

He brought the drinks, placed one in front of the empty seat. As Stefan went back to clear some more glasses, he wondered. He'd heard of veterans coming back from Iraq and Afghanistan and buying drinks to sit in memory of their deceased war buddies that had been lost in combat. But this didn't seem to be that. After all, he was talking to someone as if they were there.

The good news was that no one else seemed to notice, and he was a fully paying customer. Nothing got lost on it. Except for the drink he'd bought. If it had been something normal, Stefan might have sneaked it off himself. It ended up just going down the drain, especially after the ice melted.

Stefan didn't know quite why it stuck in his craw. But it was something he'd need to talk to Fat Man about, especially if the kid made it a habit. There are several things a good bartender has to look for, from the state of drunkenness of the patrons, to making sure they paid the tab right, and in a few cases like this one, actually keep them from mindlessly blowing money, even if the income was good for the business.

This just seemed mindless.

a fine act of repeat

There are many strange places a person can be in. Many of the solutions given for them are usually just as strange. Ever since that first trip to San Antonio, there on the Riverwalk, Jakub had become partial to the taste of the virgin Mojito. Maybe it was the lime.

Perhaps it was the mint and basil mixture. It didn't really matter. Something about it just screams out to you, and he couldn't decide what exactly it was screaming.

Everybody seemed to notice Luna. He was well aware that a grown-ass man with a stuffed toy rabbit and no kids made absolutely zero sense to anyone, but he wasn't going to let go of it. After all, it's not every day that the dead send you Priority Mail.

Has to be worth something.

He was thinking about Garry, the guy he'd met at the Statesman. Looked really rough. He appeared as if he'd needed to go to an emergency room rather than a bar, but who can know what's running through the mind of a man. Said he didn't hurt, but you'd think that he could have at least cleaned up a bit before going out in public.

Guy looked like he'd went boxing twelve rounds with a bulldozer and barely escaped with his life.

Garry hadn't had much to say to Stefan, who was tending bar. Either that or Stefan knew who he was and simply chose to ignore him. Either way, he'd asked for a gin and ginger, so Jakub had covered it. Stefan acted like he wasn't even there, and since he'd just walked in, Jakub was pretty sure he hadn't had a chance to be so drunk he got cut off. Must be some kind of bad blood between them. It happens sometimes.

He didn't have any money, or at least that was what he had said, and the way he felt, in addition to the appearance he seemed to be in... why wouldn't you at least buy the guy a drink, especially if he wasn't in the whole recovery racket that Jakub was, no matter if it was an entirely self-imposed thing. After all, Jakub wasn't the savior of the world, just himself at this moment. He knew how it was.

You don't see the things that are eating away at your skin, until they have a mouthful and you feel the pain from it. The world could be really ugly, and many times there weren't many directions to go in that would do anything useful. Jakub had been there and knew exactly what Garry was feeling.

The pain of living. It could be a dull, almost boring monotony of time all smashed together in a poultice that just wouldn't heal a damned thing.

Witch doctor medicine that simply didn't have the same effect that a good shot of juice would.

Jakub found something different, something more, and that was the thing propelling him now. Like a new driver had gotten into the racer and had the wheel. It was the only way to explain how he was able to go into a bar as an alcoholic, order virgin drinks, and still be completely cool with it and not slip.

It wasn't Jakub had much faith in the process, but rather he knew he wasn't really the one driving anymore. Everything was about a woman, as it usually is, and it didn't matter that she was physically dead. She was still out there somewhere in a form that he seemed to be able to understand and comprehend better now and it killed the drive to get drunk.

He wasn't having to deal with someone else's bullshit.

Except for Angelica, who was flittering her single fin and having a go inside the aquarium at the moment. As he watched her swim around excitedly, he sat back with his prized crystal whiskey tumbler of Diet Dr Pepper and thought about this new guy he'd met earlier.

Garry appeared to be in his 40s, maybe 50s, if you were stretching it a bit. One of the first things you noticed about him was the full brown goatee. He looked almost like the kind of guy you could see as a handyman or laborer. He really didn't have anything about him that screamed executive or any kind of high roller. The hair was a little wild even though it was short, and he had eyes that seemed slightly larger than they needed to be. Garry wasn't quite bug-eyed, but something about his looks was just a little off. Other than that, he was just a normal everyday guy that seemed to work a full day, go to the bar, then just go home to watch a game show and eat a TV dinner.

He looked like the guy that was itching with everything he was worth for a conversation, but simply didn't know how to get it started. Shyness is a bitch. Jakub knew that one very well. It had cost him a girl he really wanted once, and he hadn't forgotten it. Then again, he was on the fence with that assessment, because she hadn't liked him anyway. He didn't know she liked girls at the time.

That was a situation that went horribly wrong, and it had really hurt. What hurt even worse was the fact that he then had to see her off and on for the next three years, and when it came down to brass tacks with Veronica, she was the one he'd had to finally talk to.

Who knew she'd been Veronica's roommate? Then again, at the time he hadn't known who Veronica was for it to even matter.

Sometimes, if you keep losing big it might be time to stop playing at all.

His buddy seemed to be having issues like that as well. Things had gotten closer with Aiden since Jakub had moved to Austin, and it seemed that Jarrells spent more time floating through Austin now and that made things more fun. He always had stories with photographic evidence and was a friendly face to see in the middle of what became more of a routine to Jakub.

One of the ideas Aiden had dreamed up was some wacky adventure of buying a van, building it into some sort of a mobile man cave and traveling the country. That *did* seem to fit him, though. He was the kind of guy that would be painted as a surfer anywhere he went, even if it was mostly couches.

"Why doncha come with me?" He'd asked one afternoon as they were sipping an afternoon coffee on the tiny back porch.

"I got all of this crap goin' on," Jakub had answered.

"Sometimes it all needs to just take a break, and you do too."

"I ain't sayin' I won't think about it, I just can't do it tomorrow," he had said. But the seed was there, and he'd been thinking about the idea regularly now.

"You can't really do these things 'like tomorrow'," Aiden had replied, "They do take a little time to put together. I mean, I know people that have picked up and then never went back home, but that's the exception, not the norm. So here's the question. If you had the opportunity, and decided you might want to try it, would you?"

He hadn't even put a lot of thought into what Aiden was suggesting or what it might mean. The feelings of adventure were becoming too much to bear, like a tugging on him as if you were putting a tiny paper sailboat into a stream, so he gave the answer that went with it.

"Yeah, I totally think I could do that."

"Cool. Then I'll start saving with that in mind, and well see where we get."

"I can get on board with that. What kind of money are we talking?"

"Well," Aiden had said, leaning back in his chair, "I know that a lot of folks doing this and RVs and things like that have a steady trickle income coming in, like Social Security, or pensions, disability, things like that. But you don't have to, of course. I know that the base you'd need is about $600 a month. With two people, that gets a little more ambiguous. But let's say that it was about two grand between two people. If you bought the van outright, you don't have that bill. Then you got insurance, fuel, any travel memberships, which I *highly* suggest, and then food. Everything else is what you use to sweeten the pot. Wanna guitar? You can buy it. Wanna gadget? Pick it up."

"What happens when you get too much crap?"

"That's the beauty of it. There's a working philosophy involved. Called minimalism. So what that is basically, you find your balance of things you own. Keep 'em down to about 75% core necessity to 25% luxury. Move more things digital. All my books and photos and such are on my tablet. I store the things I like the most on the tablet, all of it's copied to the cloud. I can never really lose any of it. Just get a new device and download. Have you ever noticed that I own 2 t-shirts, and then I have this," he tugged on his pant leg, "it unzips. I don't hafta buy shorts. I just zip the legs off. I have a pair of sandals, a pair of boots. A couple hats, a light material outfit. I mean, this is my wardrobe in its entirety. I don't own anything else. If I get bored, I buy a new color of it and donate the old one to someone that can use it. Basic rule is once you hit that equilibrium, you get, you give. Everyone's happy. Zero impact."

"I'll hafta look more into that. I'm interested, just kinda ignorant on it all."

"No problem. I have a bunch of links and videos I can email ya. You might get hooked early, just sayin'. The minimalism you can start practicing now."

And then Aiden had taken off again to a new area for a week or so. That was the way he lived, almost like an alley cat, but every time he came into town, he seemed to be better educated, happier, and was always relaxed. Always had plenty of pictures to show off. Very little seemed to ever get under his skin. One of the things that Jakub liked but was also secretly jealous of, was that Aiden never seemed to get bored. He rarely had a place where he had nothing to do, and had no way to occupy his time. Even when he was doing absolutely nothing, he would be completely fulfilled.

It was maddening to watch.

He also seemed to never meet a person he didn't like. It had formed a personality in him that was plainly magnetic. People gravitated to him like a pop star. Aiden gave off a calmness and happiness that attracted the most random segment of people.

Jakub wanted to be that guy. If for no other reason than a sense of purpose.

Maybe purpose had been the thing that held him at bay. He'd been muddling along until he met Veronica. Really met her. He'd seen her before that, but the real interactions ate through him like acid, cut away to the core of him so he could see a person that wasn't so damned boring and monotonous. As far as Jakub had ever known, no one had ever paid enough attention to him to make it worth his while. Nothing he'd thought really meant anything to anyone except his sister Willie, and here this girl had admitted to practically stalking him before they really began talking.

Jakub found that he wasn't nearly as insulted as he was flattered. That might have been different if he was famous and just wanted privacy or something, but generally nobody else gave a shit, especially the people he'd *wanted* to give a shit, so this was nothing short of refreshing. Meeting Aiden was a bonus, and it had been rubbing off on him.

Monkey see, monkey do.

Angelica flittered around the tank again, trying to get his attention. He stood up to feed her. She adored blood worms, so he made sure she had a healthy supply of them. It was an easy and awesome procedure to watch, he held the tiny wad of worms up over her above the tank, and as she reached the surface, he'd drop them down to her, the single fin waving in that pattern only she could do, propelling herself up and down to get at them as they broke apart and went their separate ways in the tank.

She would be the hardest part. He didn't want to go far from her. Aiden understood that, understood why. Had suggested that perhaps if they went with the traveling idea that they limit their first trips to a few days to a week. Not too far. Take breaks.

Sure, Aiden had full service from the aquarium, his friend Sedric had arranged all of that when he gave him the fish. He'd said as much.

"If you wanna travel," Seddy had said, "Then get out there. Don't let her hold you down, that's why I bought you the service. It's pretty cheap, they do an excellent job. Live your life, son, nobody wants to see anything but for you to do well by your own standards. You've seen enough. Probably wanna see more. And ya should."

He only had a few friends, which was more than he had in Los Angeles, but they were damned good ones.

Touching Angelica on the head, he told the fish, "You're a good girl. Daddy loves you, doesn't he?" She flittered back down to the bottom of the tank happily and began looking for the loose worms she might have missed.

Jakub felt a sensation that was odd and different from anything he normally felt before. He felt it much more often now.

It was a feeling of calm and contentment.

The small rental he lived in had shaped up to be nothing short of perfect for him, almost like a little bat cave he could hide away from the world in until he was ready to face it each day. Sometimes, he didn't want to face it at all. On weekends, he generally refused to.

And that was okay.

One day, he'd get out more, adventure more. See all the new things that were waiting for him that he hadn't explored before. So many things he'd looked at in his VR goggles, but had never seen in real life. Texas alone had an entire world of opportunity in itself. He could be busy for a good long time in a van with a good friend that had enough experience to be a tour guide in his own right. But his mind drifted one more time before he decided to sleep.

He wondered where Garry was sleeping tonight. He struck him as possibly being homeless.

crying in the air

"Mack, I got somethin' I wanna ask you about," Stefan started with Fat Man.

Mackland White was the owner and boss man of The Tinder Statesman. As he wasn't the original owner, he wasn't quite sure where the name came from, but it seemed perfectly logical that the name was an homage to Stephen F. Austin, the first Secretary of State. After all, the University named after him were called the Lumberjacks, so it appeared to fit.

Mack was observing his early barkeep who was shuffling and appeared confused.

"What is it?" He asked the young man.

"I had this guy, you know, the one who comes in before happy hour and never drinks alcohol? The one with that stuffed rabbit he hauls in with him?"

"What about him?"

"Well, I was talking to him at the bar, and then he just stops the conversation and begins babbling to the stool next to him. There wasn't anything there, and he's talking to some imaginary friend. He even orders a gin and ginger. I made it, he paid for it and left it on the counter. So my question is do I make drinks for imaginary friends that I'm gonna hafta pour out later, or do I cut 'em off?"

Mack's faced crumbled for a moment.

"Gin and ginger, you said?"

"Yeah. Not usually something I get asked for here. But with this guy and all of his virgin drinks he orders every day, I thought maybe he was trying to get the real stuff without copping to it. Drunks do some strange things."

"Aw, that kid ain't a drunk. Maybe he thinks he was a drunk, but I've been in this business long enough to be able to pick out who the real drunks are. He's just a weird one, that guy. Weird, and harmless. Austin's full of them. But tell me about the gin and ginger guy. Did he ever say what his name was?"

"Umm, no. He doesn't exist. It was the kid ordering for him."

"No, did the kid ever say what his friend's name was?"

"Garry. He called his little imaginary friend Garry."

"Hollister. I figured as much."

"Come again?" Stefan asked.

"Garry Hollister. He's a regular that we had about seven years ago, and the poor bastard never left."

"What do ya mean never left?"

"Never left. Like he walked out the door and then came back and never left."

"That doesn't make any sense." *Fat Man's losing his collective shit.*

"So Garry was a regular here. Normal joe, working guy, don't remember what it was he used to do..." Fat Man was in thought, trying to recall whatever this useless piece of information was going to be.

"Ah, yes! He worked on elevators," Fat Man continued, "I thought he was a plumber or an electrician, but yeah, he worked on elevators. So he used to come in every day and order Gin and Gingers until he was just a bit too lit and take off. His wife ran out on him with some rich yahoo dude and it got even worse. But I don't think he really ordered anything else. He just wanted more gin than ginger at that point. One night he walked out about 8, right out there," he gestured towards the front of the bar with a grubby hand and finished, "Decided to have a impromptu date with the front of a truck. One of those jacked up things. Mexican drivin' was so scared he almost shit himself, but the folks on the sidewalk said he just strolled on out like he was runnin' for the bus. Dude driving never had a chance. Neither did Garry."

Fat Man leaned back and stretched. "You know what really pisses me off? Nobody gave a *fuck*. Couldn't get his wife on the phone, no family would claim him, nothin'. Guy called me from the funeral directors and somehow I ended up on the hook for this shit. Not the money, mind you, his employer paid for that, but they called me up to come pick up the box they put him in. You know how they do, ground him all up and burnt his ass down and put it in a little box. I got the box over there in a cabinet somewhere."

"Are you serious?" Stefan asked. This story was getting crazier by the minute.

"Dead serious. No pun intended. So I guess I'm stuck with the guy."

"He really never left."

"Pretty much. He never left. He's still here. In more ways than one."

Maybe it was time to show this kid a thing or two. Only the older regulars had anything to say about Garry Hollister. He had been pretty good at hiding Garry's existence from the newer patrons.

"I got some things I can show you," Mack started, "But this goes *no fucking place*, are you clear on this? The last thing I need is a bunch of those fricking television shows bugging me. I want legitimate business, not cameras everywhere and ookie spooky people bugging me for a set, and to spend the night and alla that other crap. I have enough problems in my life, and he ain't really hurtin' nothin'."

Mack cleared several windows from his monitor and produced the software for the internal security cameras.

"Okay," Mack started, queuing up the security video from the night before and sucking on his teeth, "You know how the labels on all our liquor bottles are always nice and neat, aligned perfectly to the front when it's time to leave?"

"Yeah, you make it very clear that you want 'em that way."

"You know how you don't really do that?"

"I do it. What are ya sayin'? That I don't do my job?"

"Naw, I'm saying you have a little help." He wasn't sure that the kid was taking the hint.

"I know, you usually come in and help out. I've figured that out, but I can't do everything."

"Yeah, about that. It ain't me." He felt the chill crawling down the back of his neck, and it felt like the damned air conditioner had kicked on again. Clacking the space bar on his keyboard, he froze the video at a certain point as they were closing.

"So you know how you always go and have a smoke out back when we're closin' up?" They normally ran last call at about 12:30 AM so they could shut down at 1 AM. Mitchell always went out for his cigarette at 1:05, after they'd ran the last lonely drunk out the door.

The video read 01:03:26 and Mitchell was front and center, wiping a glass with a bar towel.

"There's you. This was two nights ago. You're about to leave to go smoke. Look at the bottles on the shelves behind you. Find the ones that ain't right." Several of the bottles, including two brands of whiskey, a vodka bottle, and a gin bottle were a few that had been rotated during the evening where they weren't straight, labels off center, the vodka bottle turned with the back label facing out.

"Okay, so there's about eight of them. Sorry. Can't do *everything*."

"This ain't a pissing-down-your-back party, I'm about to show you something. So watch this." He tapped the space bar again, and Mitchell sprung back into life, finishing wiping the glass, setting it mouth down on the counter. He looked around, said something to Mack off camera, and walked towards the bin he kept his jacket in.

"There you are, grabbing your smokes and heading out. Do you remember where I was when you left to go smoke two nights ago? Because that's you talking to me." He paused the video again.

Mitchell stopped and pondered for a moment then said, "Yeah. You were back in the beer cooler working on that keg with the leaky connection."

"Exactly. Keep your eyes on the bottles. Watch *this* shit."

About a full minute elapsed in the video from the time Mitchell exited the scene. There was no one even near the bar line, no human entity in remote proximity, but they watched as the bottles began to correct themselves, one by one, from left to right, each bottle being turned by invisible hands to face front and center.

Mitchell's face drained of color.

"What the *fuck*?" Mitchell said, a look of concerned fear on his face. "What the fuck did I just watch? Are you bullshittin' me? You're joking!"

Mack grabbed a chair and rotated it for Mitchell, who looked like he was about to collapse into it. "Have a seat before ya fall down." He waited for a moment as Mitchell took in what he'd just seen. "There's more where that came from." He reached into his desk drawer for a thumb drive.

Pushing it into the computer, he clicked on another video and said, "Look at this. It was about two years ago, with Sue. That was the bartender you replaced. See? Watch the bottles again."

They watched as the lightly pudgy dirty blonde woman on the screen left the bar and again, the bottles began correcting themselves. "Same thing, right? This has been goin' on for a while. But here's the kicker, because I have another one where the bottles were all fixed with someone *behind* the bar. But that's not the one I wanna show you next."

Mack exited the video and selected another one. The one that was even more freaky.

"So," Mack began, "We thought about five years ago, when we actually started noticing this, that someone was playing a prank on us, and that was about the time I got the security camera installed and began runnin' it full time. I figured we were gonna catch the asshole that was doin' this to us. I went in and messed up about half to three-quarters of the bottles, justa be a dick. And *this* is what we got."

He pulled the video up and paused it. The timer on the corner read 02:22:22 and was dated from 2014. "Take a good look at everything before I hit play. There's nobody there, you see the bottles are all screwed up and turned wrong, and there's a lot of them. Look at one more thing. You see that length of mirror we have running head level in the bar cabinet? There's just enough lighting where you can see that there's nobody in the room. And I mean *nobody*. Angle's a bit screwy, but ya can still tell."

"Mmhmm," Mitchell murmured. It was pretty clear that he wasn't enjoying this at all, and seemed like he might be getting scared. If he wasn't before, this was certainly gonna do it.

Mack clicked the play button, and the bottles began turning two at a time from left to right, labels to the front, almost roughly, like someone was pissed off and using both hands. As the movement flowed from left to right and reached the end, there was a momentary column of white mist appeared on the screen moving from the right back to the left again.

"Shit!" Mitchell hissed, as if he'd just been poked by something.

"He ain't done," Mack said calmly. He'd watched this video so many times, trying to sort it out, that the emotion of it was almost gone, but the cold chill in his spine still wasn't. From the left side, a dishwasher rack of tumbler glasses began to levitate to the center of the bar line and the rack was turned over, the glasses being poured out onto the floor. The rack appeared to be flung down on top of them angrily as an afterthought.

Mitchell sat stunned. "Did I really just see that?" He asked, almost in a panic.

"You did, my boy. You did. That's why the bar line has the thick rubber padding on the floor now. Back then it was all hard and thick clay tile. What's under the matting when you mop the line every night. I lost that entire rack of glasses. That shit ain't cheap. That's about $250 I lost right there. He broke every fuckin' one of 'em. He tried throwing something else another time that didn't break thanks to the new mat, and at least he quit that crap."

"So, Garry Hollister," Mack continued, "He's a thing around here. I don't know how, I don't know why, or what he is, but he's here. When he gets irritated, he fucks shit up. Now you have a kid that can see 'im and talk to 'im. My advice to you, and something that can really help both of us, is to follow the kid's queues the next time he starts talkin' to thin air, and talk to Garry yourself. Treat 'im like he owns the damned bar and he's the best guy you've seen all day. Pour the damned drink and comp it. I'm willing to waste a gin and ginger a day to keep him from breaking shit. And he wasn't that bad of a guy when he was alive so he probably feels like he deserves the respect, and I ain't so sure he doesn't. Just fell on some rough times like most these folks that come in here."

"I'm not really sure what to think of all of this..."

"You don't really need to make anything from it, I don't reckon. He's not gonna hurt anyone, it's just a little odd, that's all. Usually the customers don't even notice. For me, that's a win. But see what that kid can tell ya. Pretend you're hard of hearin' or something."

living is hardest

"I can see it on your face, you're thinking again," Sarah said to Lindsey while chewing on a piece of her leftovers from the night before.

"Yeah, I have a few ideas."

"You're thinking about Tex again, aren't you?"

"Mm-hmm," she intoned, "Life is about to get *really* interesting for our boy, if it hasn't started already."

"What do you mean?" Sarah asked.

"I mean he's gonna start seeing a lot of dead people."

"Okay, I'm going to trust you on that, but you're gonna need to explain this a little more. We don't really have a lot of stuff like this in Judaism, you know. I know bupkis about it."

"Sweetie," Lindsey smiled slyly at her, "I think we've gone well *beyond* what's allowable in Judaism at this point. Time to learn how the real world works. And I meant that in the nicest possible way." She paused to sip her coffee and think.

"Here is how it all shakes out. We've both seen Veronica deceased, in an electronic device almost two years after she died, and we interacted with her.

So any questions you ever had about the idea of life after death were answered in living proof right there. The problem is that it's almost like the flu. When we're aware of the presence of the dead, that kinda sets off a little light that attracts them like mosquitoes. Jakub went farther. He's actually *in love* with her. That's a lot of emotional investment, and it's gonna light him up like a Roman candle. Jeanette's trying to re-direct him, and if it works, that's great. If it doesn't, he's gonna be a worse drunk than before, and we're gonna get to bury him."

"As morbid as this sounds, he might just off himself anyway," Sarah said, beginning to look concerned.

"Doesn't quite work that way," Lindsey answered, "Suicide isn't a good answer. He runs the risk of being stuck here, like being stuck in mud. You can't go further, and you can't go back. You're hung in between. It would take a medium to first find him and move him forward. I don't know about you, but I don't have time for that nonsense, God love 'em."

"So what are you suggesting?"

"Well, I know them both pretty well. I know Veronica really damned well. She was my roommate for over a year. She's not exactly a social butterfly, and he really isn't either. They're perfect for each other. Or would have been. I'm still kicking myself for not hooking them up at our housewarming. Remember, we talked about that."

"True, but she had Lunk, and he had that shark he was running with," Sarah finished.

"Yeah, but he just seemed to *devolve* with every chick he picked up. I would not even want to imagine who he would pick up *now*. I have an idea or two that could work, to keep him on track. Cuz he's gonna start seeing dead people everywhere, and I kinda owe it to her to keep him from getting swallowed alive if I can help it."

"*Again,* what are you suggesting?"

"I think he needs something from her, like *really* from her. If I could get those earrings she always wore, the pretty purple ones, that would be something he could wear and she'd always be with him. He has a thing for attachments. I noticed with the rabbit she sent him that he takes them very seriously."

"I don't think Jakub would look good in dangle earrings. He doesn't do the drag circuit well."

"No, silly. Not as earrings. I would have them turned into something else that he could wear..." Lindsey sharply sat up erect, "I *got* it! This is gonna be good!"

Sarah watched her leap up as she bounded towards the bookshelf. She kept a box of postcards and letters from a whole myriad of people. Veronica had sent her a postcard from San Antonio when she had gone home for Christmas while they were roommates. She'd said it was her favorite place.

Where was that?

She pawed through the box viciously until she found the card and held it aloft in victory.

"There you are!," she exclaimed with a gleeful smile, showing the face to Sarah, "The Rose Window!"

"What's that?" Sarah asked.

"Some old churchy place Veronica liked. Some love story attached to it some way. The guy was there, the girl died... it was a little too morbid for me at the time. I might have tuned out. I just know that she loved this place and there was something romantic about it to her. It's that connection I need."

"For what?"

"You'll find out soon enough."

"So you're just gonna start hiding stuff from me?"

"No, of course not. The problem is that I don't know exactly what I'm doing yet. I just know that I have to pull a bunch of things together at once and I might need to use some frequent flyer miles. Also, I have to manage to do all of this without Jakub finding out about it."

"You're starting to lose me here," Sarah said, her face almost shifting to a pout.

Lindsey scanned the back of the postcard for a single word, and she found it, close to the bottom. She positioned her fingernail under the word and flipped the card back around so Sarah could see it.

"That," she announced matter-of-factly, "That is what I have in mind. It's gonna be a little weird, but I think we can make it work."

Sarah snorted and gave a short laugh. "You're an idiot." She waited a moment to respond again, then told Lindsey, "Actually, that might not be a bad idea. That's so crazy that it actually makes perfect sense. Why the earrings?"

"Well, she wore 'em pretty much every day. Veronica was predictable enough, and for the most part plain enough that if you saw her, she normally had them on. She wasn't really a clothes girl, didn't keep a lot of them. Really simple, and *everything*, if you remember, matched the earrings. She was a purple girl. Violets, lavender, all of that. I think she got the earrings from her mother or something." She looked up in recollection, "Yeah, it was her mom. Her dad died when she was in middle school."

"And you think Mom is gonna give up the earrings she gave her late daughter. Pretty ballsy. How do you plan to pull that one off?"

"That's where the frequent flyer miles come into play. Actually, I think I might be able to get my work to cover some of it. We have a conference in Austin next month. They tried to get me to go, and with this, I just might go ahead and take them up on it. San Antonio's only about an hour away by car, and they'd be renting me a car anyway. Might as well put it to good use."

"You're going to actually go see her mother and ask for the earrings in person."

"Um, yeah…"

"Damn." Sarah snorted again, "You never cease to amaze me. You don't just have balls, you have balls of *steel*. And you're still an idiot."

Lindsey locked eyes.

"I also have a video of her daughter she hasn't seen yet."

"No…"

"Hide and frickin' watch me."

"But do you think she's really going to accept that? She doesn't even know you."

"Yes she does, I met her several times. She came out over Thanksgiving and spent a week at the apartment. She knows who I am. That woman makes some mean tamales, let me tell ya. Think about it. You're a mom who lost her husband and her kids. You have the Church telling you that they are in Heaven somewhere with little harps and wings and shit, then you get to see a video of your daughter, very dead, since you had to verify the body, but very much alive two years later. She's not in Hell, she's not in pain, and she's professing her love to a man from beyond the grave in damned near real time. You were *there*, you know what she said. I think this is a done deal. What mother in their right mind is going to be *so* selfish as not to try and fulfill their daughter's wishes after they're gone?"

"You make a good point. And I know better than to think I could stop it. You're usually on point with these things. What can I do to help?"

"Well, honestly, you have better connections than I do on jewelry because of the people you work with. I'm gonna need a good and hopefully cheap custom jeweler, and I need to source a decently well cut Herkimer diamond. Haven't quite got the design down yet, but it'll come to me. Right now I just need the source."

"A what?"

"Herkimer diamond. It does quite a few good things, and it will amplify the amethysts from those earrings. Since Veronica wore them all the time, she has her personal energy tied up in them. When the two are together, she'll almost literally be with him all the time. He'll feel her like she was right there. If he's got his girl, I'm pretty sure he *won't* have his booze."

Sarah gave her a sidelong glance. It was one of those that was always meant to be a little more than it ever appeared to be. "Can I ask a silly question?"

"Sure," Lindsey replied, bracing.

"Why do you even care? It was only a few months ago you couldn't even stand the guy."

She felt herself shrug and nod. But that wasn't the case. That had *never* been the case. *Sometimes we have to tell the sweet little lies,* she thought, *And besides, soon we'll see who the idiot really is.*

"I'm a sucker for beautiful love stories," she finally answered.

California number. Who the hell's calling me from there?

Willie only really knew one person that would have a number there, and it wasn't Jakub. He had safely returned to Austin and still had changed his number to an Austin one to throw Mom off. They had even signed it under a false name for good measure.

"Hi, this is Lindsey. I'm a friend of Jakub's," she heard the sweet voice on the other end of the line. It made her stop.

That wasn't the person she was thinking of.

Willie had been hearing about this girl for over three years, always the same things, why did she hate him so much, what had he ever done to her, oh if they could just get together. Crazy shit, ad infinitum, ad nauseam. In Jakub's estimation, it seemed like this chick pooped gold and farted rainbows. She was like the fashion model a teenage boy pasted posters of on his bedroom wall.

It hadn't mattered who Jakub was dating, even when he was engaged to the lawyer girl Mom had flabbergasted in the bathroom. He just wanted to talk about this Lindsey girl, and here she was on Willie's phone, and even saying that she was his friend, to boot.

Well, shit. This should be good.

"Gotta do something about our boy," Lindsey began. She really didn't sound the best at conversation making, and she also wasn't in the mood, apparently. Whatever the distraction was, Willie didn't feel like it had anything to do with her, so she decided to ignore it.

"Our boy? Why? Is he doing something wrong?" Willie asked. She still felt like going on the defensive, but it's not every day that your brother's former and unreachable crush calls you out of the blue to chit-chat, so she made the executive decision to play along with this.

"Not *wrong*, per se, but I wonder if maybe he doesn't need a little more observation on all our parts. Guy's got a lot on his plate. He said that he's starting therapy soon. I don't get to talk to him nearly as much as I'd like to. I guess you can understand I have... *interference.* I'm actually walking the neighbor's dog so I can make this call. You didn't hear that. Anyway, I told him the last time we talked to get into AA like yesterday. I'm not sure if you were really aware of how much he used to drink."

"He was pretty regular when we met in Vegas last time. Nothing when I saw him in San Antonio. Last time I saw him, which was a couple of weeks ago, he was still dry. He was carrying around a stuffed rabbit the last time I saw him. Won't let it out of his sight. What's that about?"

"You'll have to ask *him*," Lindsey said. "I know what that's about, but it'd be better for you to hear it from his mouth. Pretty interesting story. And I've verified it personally. He's not full of crap. Things like that are why I want to keep a close eye on him. He's been opened, so everything's about to get really interesting in his life, and I don't know that he's going to be able to hide it very well. He needs a support system to fall back on. Y'know what I mean?"

"Okay, I don't really understand all of this, but where do *I* fit into this conversation?" Willie asked.

"You are the best person I could think of to trust. You know Jakub, *really* know him, and unfortunately, not many people can say that. Including me, sadly. I wish I did. The grand scheme

I have in mind is for his benefit, and I think it's something that'll mean a lot to him, which is why I'm doing it."

"Okay, so at least give me a rundown, a vague somethin' to go on so I have an idea what to expect. I ain't great with surprises."

As Lindsey detailed the basic idea of what she had in mind, it seemed a bit out of the range to belong to a girl that had never wanted to have anything to do with Jakub.

Something in the woman's voice told Willie a horrible miscommunication was in there somewhere.

She sounded more like a starry-eyed swooning fan than a girl that hated her brother like the Hunchback of Notre Dame.

This is something I hafta see with my own two eyes.

"I don't mind helping out with that. Where do I fit?"

"I'm going to need to meet you at some point. Face to face, if that's all right with you. I guess I could tell you the story of that rabbit then, since we'll be in close quarters."

"I don't really have the wherewithal to come out to Los Angeles..."

"Oh, gosh, I'm sorry! That's not what I'm suggesting. I'm coming out there in a week or so to Dallas. Jakub said you guys live near Tyler, so I figured I'd drive that way since I'll have a rental car. I probably should've said that first. I apologize. I'm kinda new at this, I don't really ever make calls like this to people I don't really know."

"That's perfectly okay. I'd be honored to meet you. If you need anything once you get here, you have the number. Don't hesitate to call us, and we'll help ya if we can."

She seemed to relax a little on the other end of the line.

"I'm sorry," Lindsey said, "I know it's strange getting a call to meet from someone you've never heard of out of the blue like this. I just didn't know any other way to handle this."

"Oh, I've heard of ya."

"You have?" Lindsey asked, sounding confused.

"Yeah, Jakub speaks very highly of ya."

"He does?" She sounded shocked, "What does he say?"

Willie chuckled, "I'll tell ya more about that when ya get here."

"Well, that's not fair!"

"Guarantees you're comin', doesn't it?"

"I have to anyway. I volunteered for a conference I don't even wanna go to in order to come out there. Which brings to mind another question, do you have any familiarity with crystals?"

"You mean like rock crystals, or radio crystals?"

"Rock crystals."

"I don't, but a friend of mine's all into that. There's a place or two 'round here, but she goes to some shop in Dallas for hers. Something about a pyramid. If ya do a search, I'm sure you can find the place. Silver? Silver Pyramid. That's the one I'd try first. She keeps gushing about some guy there that knows all kinds of stuff about 'em and knows where they all come from. Sounds to me that's the kinda guy you're looking for to get whatever it is you're after."

"Well, I need that diamond I was telling you about. Think of it as a battery that powers everything else around it. Sorry, I have way too much experience with this, and I forget that everyone's not weird like me."

She sounded like she was apologizing too intently. Chick has some self-image issues here.

"That's okay girl, you don't need to apologize. I promise you, we'll take ya and love ya just the way you are."

It was so quiet you could hear a pin drop. Like every atom in the universe stopped spinning on a dime. Apparently that comment had hit Lindsey harder and more profoundly than Willie thought it was. Some people are just not what you think they are. In this case, she was better.

"Thank you," She answered softly, "I think that's the sweetest thing anyone's ever said to me."

"Girl, then *you* need to move to Texas. Because we mean that stuff when we say it."

"I think now if I could, I would."

"Not liking it there?"

"Well, California's my home, I grew up here, but my current situation really doesn't hold anything for me anymore."

"Oh, sweetie, I've been in that position before. I know exactly what you mean. One day I think everything will sort itself out."

"I don't know about this one. But I'll do the best I can with it. For both of them."

"I believe you will," Willie told her. After they had disconnected, she turned to Carl who was sprawled on the couch.

"You ain't gonna believe who that was." Carl grunted. That was his version of a question. "It was Lindsey, that girl Jakub's always been talking about. Y'know, the one he been swoonin' over since he moved to California?"

Carl sat up like he'd been dumped with ice water.

"How the hell'd she get this number?"

"Don't know, don't really care. She sounds perfect. Sweet as sugar, and has the self pride of an ant. Nothing like that little pollyanna cretin Jakub dragged to Vegas to meet us last year."

"Wow. So did he fuck up?"

"Dunno. She's coming out here. Wants to meet *me*."

"Make a good impression. Be a wing-girl. Do ya bro a favor."

"I don't know that she's coming out here for all that."

"Change her mind. Does she seem to be all that Jakub's said he thinks she is? I mean, keep in mind that I don't think he even knows her. He just has his impressions from afar."

"Well, we'll know what all this is when I finally meet her face-to-face. She can't bullshit me there."

i am a mouse

"So I'm thinking about grabbing a 12-pack, but I'll get two of these if you're interested." Aiden was making the call from the building of a small-time soda bottler that had cropped up in Denver. It was part of the roll through he'd set with his travel buddy Randy Carter. Randy was headed south-bound to Houston with a load he'd picked up some-where in the Pacific Northwest.

They had a little time to kill, and Randy knew about this company that sold micro-brew sodas, so there they were. Aiden knew they had distribution to Austin because the guy at the counter had said so, but he was here, at the source, and he could get any flavor they produced.

"I'm game," he heard Jakub say on the other end of the line. He sounded a little preoccupied at the moment, which was a thing with Jakub. Sometimes he zoned out, and you had to be patient with him. Lots of things had happened with that guy since he got thumped on his ass by the dead girl in the VR.

"Okay, so this is gonna be a little crazy. There's room on the back deck, right? Like a space..." He looked at the crates and calculated, "I'll get two of everything they have. We'll have plenty of time to try 'em out. There's so much here, and I know that you'll eventually wanna try 'em all. If there's anything you don't like, I'll knock 'em off."

"How many are we talking?"

"Bout 48 bottles."

"Damn! I think we can fit that. Go for it. We'll settle up when you get here."

"No need. I owe ya room and board anyway."

"No, you don't. You know you have a place here anytime you need it or want it."

"Then it's a gift from the heart."

"I can appreciate a soda gift." He heard Jakub snicker, "And I look forward to ya gettin' back in. Wanna hear all about what I missed in Colorado."

"Including the girls?"

"Especially the girls. Wait, James Bond, *what* girls?"

"Tell ya when I get there."

"Hey, pick up another case or two for Willie. I need to ride her good anyway. I'll blame you for it."

"For the kiddos?"

"Hell yeah. Wind 'em up and bend 'em out on a sugar kick. Make her crazy."

"Oh, I should probably tell ya, they use agave in these, sugar won't be nearly as much of an issue. Oh, wait. Half of 'em don't have sugar. But don't tell her that if it helps your case."

"Sounds good. Hey, anything you want me to pick up? I'm sure we'll need some food tomorrow, since it's hitting up against the weekend. What time are ya planning on gettin' in?"

"Well, it's roughly 13 hours from here to there, I think Randy's cookin' the books, so we'll probably be in before dawn. He's tryin' to hop on down to Houston before he stops to sleep. He said if he's too tired he'll park at Mustang Ridge. That ain't far from there."

"Brisket work? I can drop one in the egg out back, and it'll be ready to go when we wake up. I'll put it in probably bout midnight, let it go all night."

"Stop it, you're givin' me a woody here. I can definitely go with a good brisket. Those things are champion. You'll need a shotgun to keep the neighbors out."

"Only person I hafta worry about is Ms. Echols, and I'll take her some of it anyway. Always do. That's why we never have rent problems. I feed her the good stuff, and she gets all nice-like."

Jakub stopped, and it seemed like he was thinking.

"Hey, they ain't no way you gonna walk all those sodas down here, I know Randy can't get that trailer in here. Not really interested in getting up at 4AM, but I would if I had to. Let's do this. I'll drop the car at the gas station. That's 24 hours, and I know the owner. I think he knows who you are. You got the keys, and I'll just walk back. That way you got some-thing to haul 'em in, and ya ain't gotta walk all the way here."

"But you'll hafta walk."

"It's only like a quarter mile at best. Longer than you'll wanna carry six cases of soda. Especially if they're in bottles."

"They are."

"Well, then. It's a good idea. We'll do it. Just have him drop ya at the station. You'll see the car. It'll be line of sight of the window, under the light."

"How's Angelica?"

"She's fine. Doing the usual, swimming around and trying to be a puppy dog in her spare time. I'll let ya feed her after you drop back in. I think she's used to ya by now."

"Yeah, that'd be pretty neat! So, I'm gonna finish up here, and we'll get on the way. See ya tomorrow."

"Cool. Have a safe trip. See ya tomorrow."

Aiden went back to the desk with the attendant and said, "Yeah, so that order just grew. I'm gonna need three assortment cases of the regular sodas, and three of the agave."

The attendant looked at him like the RCA dog, so he finished, "I have three different households wanna try out your goods. Yeah, I know we can buy it in Austin, but nothing says genuine like picking it up from the source. Seriously, wouldja rather get a softly she waits for winter

beer from the store or the brewery if ya had the choice?"

"Brewery, of course."

"My point exactly!"

"We'll have that right out for you," and after ringing the order said, "That'll be $168."

"Can ya bend it? $150 cash?"

He chewed his lip. Aiden knew he had enough to cover, he usually kept around $500 hidden in secret compartments on his body, he just wanted to test his bargaining skills a bit and see if this guy would cave.

The guy tapped a few keys and said, "I have a discount I can give that'll get ya at that price point."

"I'm not gonna getcha in trouble, am I?"

He broke out into a grin, "Hardly. This is *my* place. So where are you from? You sound like you're from Texas."

Aiden felt an unfamiliar warm swelling in his chest.

Holy crap, I finally did it!

"Why, thank you very much! In fact, I'm based out of Austin now."

Something about the heating seemed to be off. One minute, everything would be nice and cozy, then as soon as Jakub was comfortable, the air would seem to turn on, and he'd be cold. But every time he checked, the air was off. It was bizarre, and it was driving him crazy, all the checking with nothing to show for it.

He liked having Aiden pop in and out like he did. Having another human around made things so much less lonely. It was hard to replace Veronica, not that he really could, nor did he intend to, but still, a fish is good for most things, but only takes you so far.

That had been a lot of his actual dealing with the Statesman, just to be in the presence of people outside of work. Work was good during the day, but then you went home, and after that, there was only so many people you could bother before it became an all out irritant.

He didn't want to date, that just felt wrong. Jakub knew people didn't understand his situation from the outside. He had no plans to hurt himself, or anything else. He was just lonely.

Still had the hormones, that hadn't gone away, they burned and stung at him. Lots of attractive women running around. It was part of the reason he went to the grocery store he now frequented. The location had a lot of young professionals, the ones that were close to walking in Santa Monica. He understood well what Aiden had been saying that time, and now instead of trying to find another one-night stand like he'd had with Ellie, he really just went to do his business and enjoy the scenery.

softly she waits for winter

Jakub had picked up a pack of cigarettes, the ones with the Indians on them. They burned slower. He really wasn't looking to smoke them all, just a couple, then keep 'em around until the next time he felt a need or desire for them.

He sat back on the cheap reclining chair he'd purchased at a second hand store and slung his leg over the arm, striking a light for the cigarette. The smoke drifted aimlessly towards the ceiling, and he watched it like he was observing a flock of doves fleeing the top rail of an apartment complex.

The way the gray gently drifted upwards, and he let his mind go numb, unfeeling, waited for all sensation to settle into a flat line before he took another drag, tasted the burnt sappy flavor of the tar on the back of his tongue. It didn't really matter, he wasn't kissing anyone tonight anyway. Nobody to lecture him on how it was all bad for him.

He still had Veronica's face in his head, the curves of her figure, the way her hair looked positioned around her face when she talked. But no matter how far he dove into that vision, no matter how warm, how full it made him feel, there was always another.

Even if no one else knew, he was completely and viscerally aware that he was a man with two masters.

Her emerald eyes and that hunger he had for them just never seemed to go away. He knew it wasn't gonna happen. No chance of it. She came with a tractor trailer load of regrets, the chances that he should have taken, even if he knew he'd just get shot down. Something always felt wrong about that whole situation, like there was something that was never said and should have been, like there was just something he was missing, and every time he saw her, it had hurt.

You always want what you can't have.

He'd rung the bell on that twice now. The commercial on the TV had a model that looked exactly like her. It was some elegant swanky diamond ad. He watched it, rewound it. Watched it two more times, then threw the remote at the television.

"Oh, fuck you." He said to the set, as if it could hear him.

Jakub wanted a drink. A real one.

He already knew what that led to for him, and he was just going to have to find another way around it. Another drag, another race to the ceiling for the streaming column of smoke from the tip of his lit cigarette, and the racing, raging clouds he blew after them.

Restlessness was the other problem. He was feeling so damned restless now, like he was supposed to be actively doing something, but he had no clue what in the hell it actually was. He'd found a decent therapist, Darcy Kitchens, and she'd come recommended by Jeanette Falkner. So far, she'd been decent, helped him get a lot of his shit out.

Darcy was pretty, herself. Probably about seven or eight years older than he was, very professional. She seemed to be damaged goods like he was, but the attraction wasn't there, and as far as he knew, that would not exactly be good. She couldn't dip into patient ink, and that was what he was... a patient. So it was a good and safe ground.

She knew about both of them. They had talked about his inability to pursue the things he wanted, how that was connected with the Queen Bitch DuJour, and how perhaps his current no-contact solution regarding his mother was probably the healthiest option. Darcy was supportive on all counts. She told him that he would eventually have to deal with both of these women that were unknowingly locked into a back and forth struggle over his heart.

One of them was alive and didn't speak to him voluntarily. He couldn't get to her if he wanted to. The other was beyond the grave, and couldn't do much to fix the issue anymore. He obviously couldn't get to *her* anymore. Both of them were connected tighter to each other than either was connected to him.

It was a colossal fucking mess.

He hadn't spoken to Lindsey since he left California. Something about her just unleashed pure animal in him. It was like those industrial magnets. No matter what else was going on, who else was involved, she found her way back in without even trying. There was no question that he was crazy about Veronica to points that were unhealthy, but he'd wanted to grab Lindsey and plant one on her right in front of Sarah and let the world burn down into a flaming, ashy mess around them. He realized it would be like those cartoons where the skunk spent thirty minutes chasing and stalking a poor cat to share his version of romance, *parfait magnifique.*

It would probably end with a moving truck outside the precinct, and him inside it, behind bars. You can't just walk up and kiss girls anymore, even if you know them well. So that was pretty much off the table.

Better to finish the cigarette, lick all his wounds, and go to sleep.

Besides, there was brisket.

fields of paper flowers

This Jakub guy was one hell of a special snowflake.

Actually, that sounded worse in Darcy's head than she'd meant it to. He was just very different, bless his heart, and most of that was because he'd had a very different experience than anyone else she'd ever heard of.

Most intuitives have a hard enough time dealing with the reality of other realms, but in this case, a complete outsider, someone who normally would never have been attuned to the paranormal in any capacity, developed an intimate relationship with someone who was already dead.

Physically, anyway.

The experience had bent him into the person he was now, at this moment. The fear from everyone else that really knew him was that there would be more to come. The danger with interacting in the worlds beyond was the connection, and that connection would become visibly apparent, almost like a marker, to those that were beyond.

His love affair with a young girl he dreamed of being with in life, and then truly connecting to her beyond the veil, well, that had lit him up like bright runway lights after a fog. Everything had been uncovered, and the usual blocking mechanisms had been removed. The greatest problem at hand was that he didn't know any of that had happened, so Jakub would be totally unprepared for many of the things that were going to start happening next.

And this was where Darcy had come into play. When Jeanette Faulkner had called her and said she had a special case that required her attention, she knew it was going to eventually go paranormal.

Jeanette doesn't make normal calls. When she's on the phone, something wild is going down.

She had gone balls-to-the-wall with it, and within the first two minutes of the conversation, Darcy was without a shadow of a doubt that Jeanette Falkner was not one to take a 'no' as an answer that day. Nor was she willing to select anyone else. After all, Darcy had been her protégé, and the level of information and skill she'd learned at Jeanette's hands still sometimes astounded even her.

As far as Jakub had known, Darcy was just going to be his therapist, someone to talk to about his dealings with a dead girl in a piece of electronics. Honestly, the first vision she'd had in her head was the little girl from Poltergeist inside of the TV. It was benign compared to some of the things *she'd* seen.

Today's session had given her all of the warning signs. Jakub had talked about a new guy he met at the bar, and how some people were strange because every time this new friend, Garry, had come around, he felt like they had turned the air conditioner on.

"He's weird. I mean, every time he gets near ya, it feels like you got next to a block of ice. But it doesn't seem to affect him at all."

"Ice, you say?"

"Yeah, it's weird, he just seemed to take the air conditioning with him. Never seen anything like it."

"You said you buy him drinks?"

"Yeah, he likes gin and gingers. I guess everybody has their thing. Never tried one myself. But he never drinks them. I buy 'em for him, and he doesn't touch them. I guess he's nervous and drinks them after I leave. Some people are just weird like that. I give him his peace."

"So you just buy him drinks every day."

"I was. Barkeep says my money's no good for him anymore, and they just give them to him when I order 'em now. But that's the thing. They won't give him a drink unless I ask for it, which totally seems strange to me. Lotta weird stuff in this world."

You have no idea, yet.

Darcy paused a minute to put the pieces together. If the guy was cold to be around and couldn't drink his drinks, then he was a ghost. Jeanette was right. The interactions with Veronica had turned him into a medium. In the wrong hands, and without information, that was dangerous. He could get pegged as a schizophrenic or worse, and never know that anything at all was amiss.

"What bar did you say this was at?"

"Tinder Statesman."

She wrote the name on the top of her session notepad and circled it, let the guy get into his small talk again so he didn't realize just yet what she was thinking about. Thankfully, their time was almost up, so she politely closed up shop with Jakub and gently shooed him on his way.

Once Jakub had safely departed, she pulled up her laptop and began searching for the bar. It was easy to find, thank goodness this guy had a social media strategy. There he was on the website, a pudgy smiling bearded man, Mackland White, Owner. Hopefully this would be as easy as she anticipated.

The drive had taken about 15 minutes from her house. She arrived at the Tinder Statesman with a sense of business and walked through the front where a man in his late 30s and a beard was wiping glasses and greeted her while surveying her with his eyes.

"I'm looking for Mackland," she asked.

"Trying to serve something?"

"Uh, no. What do you mean? I'm here to talk to him about something personal."

The man raised his eyebrows and let out a low whistle. "How the hell did he pull *that* one off?" He murmured lowly, but she'd heard it.

"Excuse me?"

"Nothin', just thinkin'. I'll go get him."

The barkeep returned with the fellow from the picture. He looked only slightly better in person.

"Mackland White," the man said, introducing himself.

"Hi, I'm Darcy Kitchens, could we speak in your office?" He immediately seemed to go on the defensive. "I'm not sure what you might be dealing with, but I'm pretty sure it's not anything you're thinking of. Look, let me put your mind at ease a bit. I'm Jakub Riser's therapist."

"The kid with the rabbit?"

"Yes."

"God, please tell me he didn't die!" He asked, looking exasperated.

"What? No, he's quite fine. But I do want to talk to you about some things he's been telling me, and I'm pretty sure you don't want to have that discussion out here in the public way, if you know what I mean."

"Ah. Sure. Follow me," Mackland said, leading her to the back of the bar and into an office that had seen better days. He pulled up a chair for her and let her get comfortable.

"I'll get to the point. I'm not just a therapist, I deal with the paranormal." She saw him recoil and decided to go further. "I like quiet. I do real work, I don't do the showmanship garbage, so I'm not here for that."

"Okay, so where do I become involved?"

"Garry. That's where you become involved." She saw him shrink back slightly, trying to regain composure.

"So where is Garry buried?" Darcy asked.

Mackland exhaled. "He's not. He was cremated, and I have his cremains in the file cabinet over there. I haven't had the heart to do anything with them. He loved this place. Nobody else wanted him, so I kept him. What has the kid told you?"

"Nothing that he realizes he's told me. In fact, he has no idea I'm here talking to you, and for now, I'd like to keep it that way. Talking to you isn't exactly legal. You can appreciate my desire for discretion."

"Sounds fair to me."

"Jakub is becoming a physical medium. What that basically means in layman's terms is that he sees people that have died and are stuck on our plane as solidly and as literally as you're looking at me, and I'm looking at you. To him, there's no difference. Problem is, he has no clue he even has that skill yet. You know Garry's dead. I know Garry's dead. Jakub thinks he's a guy that doesn't care about his appearance and never has enough money for a drink. To him, Garry's a friendly Wimpy of alcohol. That's the reality of it."

"So what are you suggesting? How does this involve me?"

"How attached are you to Garry? Because I think it would be a great idea for him to finally go home where he can get some rest."

"And where is this 'home'?"

"Not on this plane. He really needs to be crossed over before a bunch of jerkoffs in leather jackets and TV shows realize he's here and start calling the Film Commission."

"Now you're speakin' my language, lady. When do ya wanna do this?"

"When's your slowest time?"

Mack rubbed an imaginary spot on the table with a hairy thumb as he thought. "My slowest time, believe it or not, is Saturdays around 3PM. Normally it's us and the mice then until about 4:00, then it starts up. We don't even see the kid on the weekends. He only shows up during the work week."

no one's biting

The scene before Jakub was both upscale and modern. It looked like cream marble slabs had been laid one on top of another in disjointed stacks in a way that was both artistic and aesthetically calming.

It screamed *luxury*. This had to be a hotel.

Ah. Well look at that! It's a hotel.

To the right in large metal letters, the words RADISSON COLLECTION on a brick-faced wall, and in front, in similar raised stenciled letters, OLD MILL BELGRADE. He had no idea what the Cyrillic characters were underneath it. He was pondering how he'd gotten there when a lovely brunette in a white top with khaki-colored jacket and pants floated in like a ghost behind the counter.

The concierge greeted him with a good evening and asked his name.

"Jakub Riser," he told her. The girl drew her finger down a few documents behind the counter, looked up at him with a warm smile and said "Yes, you are over in our dining area at OMB. Walk with me, please."

The concierge led Jakub along a marble-tiled walkway imagined being a corridor of sorts, chairs staggered in logical artistic order with large plate windows allowing the darkness to be seen from the right, lights shining through in a spectacular display.

As they entered into darker and more intimate dining area, with deeper browns and angular columns, glassware and place settings meticulously arranged in show room displays, patrons also parked in positions engaged in conversations undecipherable to him.

For some reason that eluded Jakub, this was the first time he'd thought to look down, and realized he was formally dressed, perhaps from the soft feel of the shirt he was wearing.

French cuffs! I always wanted to wear a shirt with French cuffs. Never could afford 'em.

The shirt was a soft lavender with a deep navy suit that almost appeared black. Looking again, he thought to check his cuff links. He hadn't owned a pair before. They were deep purple amethyst butterflies.

Why do I have butterflies?

He remembered once he had a butterfly stuck in his cubicle at work. As a matter of fact, he'd taken it to Austin to his new job.

They moved closer to the end of the aisle, a more intimate table currently seating a couple, a man that looked like a male model, and a delicate woman with a buzz cut and her back to him. She only casually acknowledged his presence as they approached.

The couple were a heavily tattooed male with a muscular build and a neat, close blond haircut. Jakub couldn't decide if he was a boxer or a cop. His suit was streamlined with a flamboyant-looking tie. The woman at his side also had short hair that reminded Jakub of Audrey Hepburn. Her baby blue dress was lace-like, extending to the neck in a Victorian fashion. As she stood, he realized her facial features were Slavic, Russian, he presumed. A thin, single black rose was tattooed up the side of her neck along her right ear. Then Jakub's eyes drifted.

She was blessed.

The man's face broke out in a grin as she shook her head with a smirk and said, *"Men."* She then motioned to the seat at the end of the table next to her and said, "Here, Mr. Riser. Welcome home."

"Stanton," the man at the other end introduced himself. He looked as if he'd escaped the cover of a *Gentleman's Quarterly* magazine. "I like to be conservatively fashionable. At least I make the effort." The boxer cop guy raised his eyebrows in irritated disbelief, but said nothing.

Jakub felt the presence behind him, but found that suddenly he couldn't turn his head to more than a 45-degree angle to each side. He couldn't see who or what was behind him.

"It appears that everyone that needs to be here, is here," said a feminine voice, almost like music. "I represent Veronica Salazar, you two of course have Jakub here, and... others."

The woman to his left nodded lightly, although she looked simply lost in thought.

"So why does *he* get two? What makes him so special?" Stanton said, a concerned look on his face.

"I make him special. Plus, they wanted to work together, and I see no reason to deny that."

"Why don't you come and have a seat?" Stanton asked, coaxing her.

"That's okay, here's fine. I don't need to be in front of him yet. He can't see me, and for now it's best that way."

He felt the hand rest on his left shoulder, and all that could be seen was slender fingers tipped in a wine colored nail polish. She smelled of French lavender.

"I don't really understand what's happening here," Jakub said, "I also don't understand why I'm here, specifically. I feel like I'm having a moment out of *The Matrix*."

"That's okay, sweetie," the voice behind him said, "You're dreaming. Just be quiet and let the grownups talk. We'll get to you in a minute." She paused and finished, "God, that felt good. I'm not gonna be able to say *that* for much longer."

"I know what you're trying to do," Stanton said pointedly, "I get it. And you have every right to, because it's written in the paperwork here. But he's missed *two* convergence points. This looks more like a checkmate to me, and I don't see why he's being allowed to open up in the first place. What the hell have these two been doing?"

"You don't get to pin that on *us*," the tattooed man spoke, "We're a recent assignment. Where he's going, he needs all the help he can get." He held a fist up and turned to Jakub. "I apologize. We're being rude to you, and I think there are a few things that you can be told on a need-to-know basis for the moment. I'm Hester. *James* Hester, if ya wanna get technical, but nobody calls me anything but Hester. This is my partner, Shelaine. We were married when we were carnate. Crossed over during Operation New Dawn. Damned IED. We're Army Airborne. Or were."

"Once a paratrooper, always a paratrooper," Shelaine said.

Ah. So they aren't cops, they're military. Now that makes sense.

"I didn't know a husband and wife could work together," Stanton hissed, "Isn't that against the law?"

Hester eyeballed him with obvious restraint, "We were in the same vehicle, not the same chain of command. Where the hell's all this saltiness comin' from, pretty boy? We don't have nothin' to do with you. Besides, we've passed. What jail do ya think you could take us to? My commander's probably banging his mistress right now. Been a decade. He doesn't care."

"Children, please," the voice behind him said lightly, "Mr. Stanton here has his delicate panties in a wad because I found the perfect guy for his charge. He's a little jealous, and that's understandable."

Stanton's face crumpled in disgust.

Jakub observed the girl sitting to his left. She eyed through the paperwork that everyone was talking about and seemed to voluntarily ignore the maelstrom going on around her. He had no idea what was on the papers, or really what they had to do with, but apparently they were important.

She had a lovely European-looking face with reddish hair that had been shaved down to a stubble. Large, thin gold hoop earrings hung in her ears to accent the outfit she was wearing, a gold-rimmed white cocktail dress. He could see her right arm was tattooed down to the knuckles, a lotus flower blooming on a delicate right wrist. She flipped another page and shifted her body more in Jakub's direction.

He noticed that her legs were crossed, left over right, and on the left shin was the tattoo of a butterfly.

Butterflies. Everywhere now.

"Checking out the merchandise?" Stanton spit caustically.

Heston smiled mischievously, "What normal man *wouldn't*? My god, look at those legs!" He was obviously trying to turn the cranks on Stanton. Shelaine snickered and playfully punched him on the arm. The girl grinned, still studying the papers.

She looked up and into Jakub's eyes with her own, the soft blue color of arctic glaciers, and he felt like he'd been hit in the face. She looked so damned familiar. Smiling in amusement, she lightly shook her head and said, "Sherilyn Fenn."

"What?"

"You're wondering who I look like. Sherilyn Fenn. It's all I heard from the time I was about 17. Don't even try to see it myself, but they say it's the eyes." Flashing a bright grin she said, "Made it really easy to get a date, I can tell ya that. I'm Corisande. You can call me Cori. Everybody else does." Turning to Stanton she added with a pointed finger, "Except you, asshole. I'm *Miss* Corisande to you."

"If it's not rude, can I ask how you passed?" Jakub asked.

She eyed him with a blush, "Car accident. I'd had a little too much to drink, and I was, ahem," she looked upwards with an embarrassed grin, "*distracting* the driver. Didn't end well. He got ejected and survived. I didn't have anywhere to go. You don't want to see what I looked like. I'm sure he

had a hard time explaining his state of undress."
Hester immediately snorted and lurched forward in
laughter.

Cori choked and said, "That came out wrong..."
Shelaine was the next to lose her composure and
begin laughing hard. "Dammit," Cori said, "I can't
stop. Shit. I'll shut up now." She was waving her
hand in front of her face like a fan, trying to regain
herself.

"You, my dear," Hester said, still snickering, "Get
the prize for Best Exit. I don't know many people
that can come close to that one."

"So," the voice behind Jakub spoke, "It's not that
he's being allowed some special privilege from the
Grand Poobah or anything, the fact is he opened up
when he spent all of that time talking to Veronica
after she passed. There's a connection, and since
neither of them want to break it, there is no reason
to do so. Because of that little nugget, he's open. It's
unavoidable. Might not have been what he signed
up for, but it's what he got. In my opinion, it fits. But
you all know I'm biased to begin with. We just need
to get the maximum benefits for everyone involved.
You can call it damage control, but I call it
opportunity."

"Still," Stanton started.

"Still, have ya stopped to consider that the only
reason you're even here is because your charge is

good at this stuff? She's a great mentor, he *needs* a great mentor."

"Where is Veronica, anyway?" Cori asked.

"She's in Review. She'll be around soon enough."

Cori picked up a single page out of the disheveled stack again and scanned it. She was deep in thought and had a concerned look on her face. "Okay, so I hafta advocate for my peep here. You know she's still in love with him." Cori was looking intently at whoever this woman was behind him.

"I know." He heard the soft answer, almost milky and sad.

"No, I don't think you get what I mean. I was assigned to her right before the first convergence failed, and she's been broken ever since. Hairline fractures are still fractures, and they hurt like hell." Cori rapped the page with an index finger, "Y'know, there's history here, and there's a distinct possibility of a third C point. I think I have a scenario that will work out for everyone involved."

Hester leaned forward, "Do you have your charge's paperwork?"

Cori nodded, "Always."

"And what does it say about this proposal of yours?" Shelaine asked.

"Nothing, yet. Not that's specific. That's kinda why we're here, isn't it?"

"But your charge is not. Only Jakub."

"I have approval to make the change I have in mind, I *promise* you."

Hester looked over at Jakub and said, "Whiteline it. Let's see it."

"Okay, gimme a moment," Cori said, separating out one page from Jakub's paperwork, and one from the stack she'd brought. She used her finger to scan a paragraph on the paper from her charge, and Jakub saw the letters rise above the page about a millimeter and then rearrange. He couldn't read the words from where he sat, but they remained, floating over the paper and stayed in place.

Cori then took the document from Jakub's paperwork, found the place she desired, and repeated the motion again. She slid both across the table to Hester, who looked at them with Shelaine peeking over. Shelaine lit a smile over her face and nodded as Hester whistled out loud with raised eyebrows.

"Girl, you're *slick*. I love this. A little out of the ordinary, but it's as clean as you're gonna get, and I think it'll be satisfactory to all parties concerned." He stood to pass the papers over Jakub's head quickly into the hands of the woman behind him.

Jakub tried to get a glimpse of the writing on the documents, but the paper appeared to be either too thick or a material he couldn't see through.

The voice behind him said, "This is beautiful. I can get an agreement to this." She paused, then

Jakub felt the intense rush as she leaned down behind his ear and huskily whispered, "Do you trust me?"

The feeling of unbridled electricity ripped through his body like an eruption. Then he felt self-conscious, realizing that he was now fully erect, and his dress slacks were making no effort to conceal that fact.

"Hey, *easy*!" Hester shifted quickly, brusquely scolding the woman behind Jakub. "You can't do that to a guy, get all close in on him and start whispering like that. I know you didn't have any of that kinda experience before, but that's a *sexual* thing. You'll have that poor bastard humping everything including the sofa like a dog in heat. Back up a little. He's not deaf."

"Sorry," she seemed to recoil in horror, "sorry. I guess I just got carried away, that's all. So, Jakub, do you trust me?"

"I don't know who you are."

Hester's eyes immediately tracked to the woman behind Jakub. The look on his face indicated that response did not go over well.

"You should trust her," Hester said, "She's definitely not going to steer you wrong."

"I have to have your approval before changes can be made to your documents."

"What are those documents, anyway?"

"Life Plans," Cori said, "Everyone makes one before they carnate. Before you're born. It's kinda like a contract that spells out the major things in life you're supposed to do, connections you're supposed to make, and it has vectors for if you do everything according to your Plan, and the craptastic adventure life will become if you don't. Has a exit point potentiality section, all of that. My proposal helps fix one thing that got severely screwed up and wasn't supposed to. It's a fix that has a critical impact on several other people, but it doesn't affect things when you get here. It's a good thing. I promise."

I know what I want.

Shelaine looked Jakub in the eye and then said, "Don't we have…"

Hester looked down at the bottom of his page and tapped with his finger.

"Doesn't change anything. And we can tell him that." Looking at Jakub, Hester said, "We *are* allowed to tell you this. And you're allowed to remember it when you wake up. When you exit, Veronica is your hard-coded Retrieval Agent."

"What does that even mean?" Jakub asked.

"When you die, when you exit, Veronica will be there to pick you up. You won't be alone, she *will* specifically be there, no matter what."

Jakub nodded, as hope began to well up in him. There was so much more to life and everything attached to it than he ever imagined. All these people, and all these plans, and all this stuff he never knew was even involved.

Jakub turned to Shelaine, "You said 'Welcome Home' when I first got here. Why? I've never been here. We're in Serbia, right?"

"Yeah," she said with a smile, "Basic geography, Belgrade is in Serbia. You're Bohemian. This is part of the region that ethnic group comes from. So technically you're in the land of your fathers, which I guess is the best way to say it."

"Russian?" He asked her.

"My origins are. I'm third generation American, I guess. Belorussian, if you want to be technical. Being born in America made me 'Shelaine' instead of 'Svetlana'. Might have been different otherwise."

Hester slid the papers back across the table to Cori and said, "With *those* tits, they could have named you Igor and I'da still married ya."

Shelaine snorted and said, "Shut up. You're not helping."

"The question is, Mr. Riser, do you approve the changes in your plan?" The lady behind him asked. He didn't feel threatened, which was a good sign.

"I approve them," Jakub said, "And are we just meeting here?"

Hester held up a hand to summon the attendants that were just within sight. A young man appeared and motioning towards Jakub, Hester requested, "Cubano Mojito. I would like a Salto, please."

Shelaine blurted, "Ah? Paklena Pomorandza, please."

Jakub noticed that while they were ordering, the letters on the pages had sunk down into the papers. It looked like a done deal, then.

Cori was sorting through her charge's paperwork again and waved the young man off. Stanton appeared to be sucking sour grapes, wishing he was somewhere else.

"You are excused, Mr. Stanton. I'm certain you have other things to do right now. Wouldn't want to keep you," the lady behind Jakub said. Stanton wasted no time exiting with a huff. It was obvious he really hadn't wanted to be there.

"That guy," Hester said, "Who put the stick up *his* ass?"

"He's harmless. Just cranky and jealous. They assigned him to his wife he had when he was incarnate. It's a bad move, if you ask me. He was this way back then, too. She's supposed to have another partner, though, and he's intentionally screwed up the last *five*. You're supposed to help your charge, not sabotage them. I have the perfect guy for her that would give her the excitement she needs, but also treat her well. He's havin' none of it. Keeps going the way he is, and I'm gonna rat 'im out."

"What would they do?" Shelaine asked.

"Reassign him," Cori said, "Probably to somebody that likes dirt and skateboards. That'd really irritate him."

"I think I know the answer to this," Jakub began, "but what's a charge?"

"A charge is a living person," Hester answered, "We're usually called guides, at least in all those woo-woo circles running around. Every living person has one, or more, in your case. They kinda oversee what is going in the charge's life, make sure that things are going at least in the general arena of what's in the Life Plan, and when things get hairy, we can step in on request and help re-align. I guess in your world it'd be like a project manager. On this side, we're normally called advocates or representatives, the term doesn't matter as much as the function. The nice lady behind you is acting as an advocate, but she's actually a protector."

"What's the difference?" Jakub asked. He was answered by the lady behind him.

"Among the living, or the 'woo-woo circles' as Hester put it, I would be called an angel. Also known as a protector, and why Stanton isn't crazy about me but knows to sit down and shut up when I speak."

"Just suffice it to say," Cori said, "When *she* shows up, shit's about to get real."

"Couldn't have said it better myself," Hester finished.

until you realign

"Mom's up to her usual tricks, but I keep deflecting her. She ain't got your number yet, and I think she's figured out ya left Cali, but she still doesn't know where, so I play stupid for the most part. Good thing we changed the name on your phone. Keeps trying that meltdown tactic with me. You know the one where she cries and acts like the world's ending. I swear that woman cries so many damned crocodile tears that she coulda filled ponds on the Crocodile Hunter."

"I'd pay to see that. Pay more to watch her wrestle a crocodile. Call Florida. We might could arrange that."

"Florida has alligators, not crocodiles."

"As long as they finish their dinner, I don't care what they are."

Sad thing was, Jakub wasn't joking. But neither was she. Their mother was a right pain in the ass just as a general rule, even more when she felt she wasn't getting her way. Both Willie and Jakub were determined that the days of Mom getting her way in anything involving them were over, and that had made her about as fun to deal with lately as fighting off a pack of angry monkeys with a plastic spoon.

"How are things with ya? That fella Aiden still popping through?" Willie asked.

"Yeah, he's headed back this way now. He been in Colorado for a minute. I reckon it went pretty well, because he called me from a soda brewery in Denver wantin' to know what soda flavors I liked. Micro-brew or something. You know how he is, he has to go investigate everything."

"You know he's gonna run into the wrong girl one day, and that boy'll be parked good. She'll ground his ass."

"That, or he'll haul her off with him. Not like it'd be a bad thing. Him finding interested girls is *not* an issue."

"Oh, no. I ain't saying it's a bad thing, just that he's gonna get got one of these days. The other thing I wanted to talk to ya about, and yeah, we're back to Mom... You might wanna check your credit reports."

"Oh, shit. What's she scheming now?"

"This one's pretty sick. She started some side accounts and investments in my name, but they weren't from me, in fact, it was a full on battle for me to get access to 'em. I think she's actually shaving money off of Vera and hiding the change in there. Was. I have access to 'em now, and we're just gonna let her keep her dirty work up. Pretty sure she got started on that path because like an idiot I told her what me and Carl are doing. You know me, I don't get out that much, and this place ain't that big, and I guess I just can't shut the hell up sometimes. So we're gonna sit on it and let her continue."

"Rather than just sic the authorities on her?"

"Bitch has to die sometime. I figure I let her fill it up, make as much money as she can, and then I'll hand it back to Vera at some point. Let that poor girl be free. She already wasted enough time with Mom, and if I know Mom, that ain't a healthy relationship. Dealing with her is like gettin' caught in an electrified spider web." Willie could hear the tension on the line as Jakub processed what she was telling him.

"Okay, I get that plan. I'll look at everything and see what's going on. Problem is if I touch any of it, my location's wide-ass open."

"Not necessarily. Just see if anything's been done you ain't familiar with. Let me know, get what information you can, and we'll figure it out from there. Plenty of ways to work around this crap of hers. At least I've been able to keep her off your phone line. So if she kicks her heels up and croaks, you wanna know about it? Be part of it?"

"Not really. I think I've had all the dealings with her I want. I ain't got nuthin' against Vera, so I'd be glad to help any way I can after that, but Mom can fuck herself. She's hurt enough people in her life."

"What about you? You been doing any future preparations? Like IRAs at work, anything like that?"

"Nah, just got the savings account. Why?"

"You need to be making something off of that, y'know? Somethin' more than what you're doin' now."

"I get interest."

"Probably not shit, though. We got started on this whole investing thing last year, and it's been payin' off. Get better kickbacks, and I think we'll be sittin' much prettier by the time we boot the kids out the nest. You know little people can invest now."

"Midgets? Or children?"

"No, jackass. Folks that ain't rich, like us. We got into that whole micro-investing thing. Carl got really excited about it, probably more than I did before I learned all about it. Now he fills the pot and I manage it. Part of my checks go into it too. Did a bunch of trimming on what we was spending and it's looking like it's all headed the right way now."

"Look at you. Moving to Wall Street anytime soon? Watching too many movies about it?" He was trying to tug at her chain, but she was serious. Kid needed to get a better handle on his crap. After all, looking after her little brother had been a thing for a few decades now.

"Hell, you should bring Aiden here sometime. We can go over it. Better yet, ask him about it when he gets into town. He probably already knows about all that stuff and we were late on the bus. You know how he is, he seems to know everything about everything before everyone else. Thank God he doesn't act like it."

"Yeah, he's probably about one of the most selfless people I know."

"Hey, I got a call from a friend of yours the other day. Oddly enough they want to meet me and not you. At least not yet."

"Aiden?"

"Nope. We were just talking about him. Why would I ask you about him if he was the one who called? C'mon, man! Naw. Somebody else. Someone you'd never expect, and I ain't telling you who. I promised."

"Then why fricking bring it up?"

"Because it's my job as your big sister to watch out for you, and torture the livin' piss outta ya any chance I get. But this sounds like it's a good thing. I'll drop more hints later if I'm able to. I know you love surprises just as much as I do."

"Which is not at all," Jakub said.

"Yeah, but ya gotta trust your big sissy, kid. I'll look out for ya. If I think this is shady or jacked up in any way, I'll drop a damn hammer on it."

"Oh, wait. Speakin' of Aiden, I mentioned the microbrew. He hates your kids. He's bringin' 'em sodas. Like a case."

"That ain't hatin' *them*, that's hatin' me. Should I take offense to that?"

"Do ya *want* to take offense to that? I mean, it's a free country and all."

"Now, you tell that handsome lookin' mother trucker..."

"Sounds like ya might have a lil thing for 'im there."

"Yeah. I do." She couldn't help but laugh. "Guy's as sweet as can be, well-mannered, *easy* on the eyes. Hell, when he stayed here that week workin' with Carl, I thought old boy developed a man crush on 'im. I think he'd move him in if he could get the chance. Guy ain't afraid of work. Good friends that are worth a shit are hard to find. Lot you can learn from that guy. But don't short yourself. There's a lot he can learn from you, too. I think that might be part of the reason you still see so much of him. Besides, he's pretty much family now. We hafta cobble it together where we can."

"So when he calls back and you guys meet up or whatever, you're gonna hafta tell me how it went down. What was his name again?"

Willie let out a chuckle, "Nice try, Buster. You shoulda known that wouldn't work. I ain't telling' ya shit until I need to."

He didn't need to know that it was a *she*, not a he. Besides, his little head would have exploded.

"I'm gonna worry about this for the next month," Jakub moaned.

"You don't need to worry until I tell you to worry. I think everything is under control. Nothing to worry about, nothing to see. You just keep working on keeping yourself straightened out. I feel good about all this."

"Glad somebody does."

"When are you guys bringing the torture juice to my children and making me wanna kill ya?"

"When's good?"

"Well, we're tied up this week and next, how bout Saturday week? We can grill something. Don't let that Aiden get lost again. Bring his ass too. Kids love him. He's their hero, next to you."

stop at every station

It all started with Roger.

All of this mess, all of this crap, started with him. Dude was an absolute freak. He'd first shown up when she was about 12, and she'd woke up to the inside of her left thigh being caressed by fingers, a stroking up and down. It was a strange sensation, and she thought at first that her mother was playing a prank on her, because her dad would never dared to touch her or behave that way.

When she opened her eyes, she wasn't prepared. She also didn't expect the bloodcurdling scream that was trying to force its way from her lips, but she discovered to her horror that she couldn't scream.

He sat on the edge of her bed, his hand on her thigh and a very crazy look in his eye. The right eye. Because the left side of his face was crushed in at the upper jaw and that part of his face looked like a busted bluish balloon.

She spent the better part of two months trying to avoid him, and he popped up everywhere. At school, in public, in her bedroom. He only got close enough to touch her when she was in bed asleep, and it was always the same perverted stuff. He was a creep that scared her, and seemed to enjoy doing it.

She tried talking to her parents, Mom wouldn't discuss it, and Dad said she was just going through the stress of adolescence. Neither of them were any help at all. She tried talking to a friend at school, and that went horribly wrong. After that, she was called "the crazy girl", and no one wanted to have anything to do with her at all. Kids are horrible and ruthless when they have a walking target.

Then he started invading her dreams.

She didn't even want to recall those. It changed everything. It changed how she looked at men, with the exception of Dad and a small handful of other males. And since Dad had been little to no support at all, sometimes she had trouble trusting even him.

Jeanette was the first to truly sense something was wrong and took notice. And it was Jeanette who first explained that there was more to the world than just what the normal eye could see, and Lindsey was blessed with eyes that saw much more than normal.

That wasn't good enough. An explanation wouldn't make the boogeyman go away.

She learned from Aunt Jeanette about how to blockade herself against Roger. Her older mentor taught her about black salt, bordering, cleansing with sage, and tar water. She learned the beginnings of what would become a study in crystals and what their molecular structures could help provide.

Sarah called it her 'rock collection', and it was usually the butt of many jokes that were usually at her expense. Lindsey just blew them off, no matter how irritating they were, because those were the things that had kept him at bay, as well as others like him.

Every item of jewelry she owned had a rational motive that only she understood. She taught Veronica a lot about dealing with crystals when they lived together as roommates.

Veronica had taken to the whole idea like a duck to water, since she was in the sciences and a degreed scientist to begin with. She saw immediately the possibility and even the probability of what Lindsey was saying and to an extent researched it further, settling on amethysts as her primary gem of choice.

All of that only had a slight bearing as to why Lindsey was here, sitting in the less than optimal chair bench contraptions at baggage claim in Dallas-Fort Worth International.

Soon she would lug her bags to the car rental office and prepare for two luxurious days of smiling, waving, and handing random imprinted objects to people she hadn't wanted to meet. She was only attending because she would have the next day off to go meet Jakub's sister.

To say that she was less than prepared for either would be an understatement. The only difference was she'd done the former to get a free ticket to the latter. Sometimes you have to make little sacrifices here and there to accomplish your goals.

There was one place she'd wanted to go, as Lindsey had done her research on all the crystal shops in the area and the one she'd talked to in Richardson where the nice young man seemed to have plenty of what she was looking for.

A Herkimer Diamond.

Sarah had proven to be utterly useless in anything that was related to this venture, even after that whole doe-eyed spew of how she 'had her back' and 'would help any way she could'. Basically, she either couldn't because she was too lazy, or wouldn't because she was quite double-faced and undependable.

She had her good moments, but much of the time it was all going to go Sarah's way, like the parties Lindsey never wanted to go to. Somewhere in there would be a guy or a girl that would gravitate to her, against her will, then Sarah would get too lit and run at the mouth. Then there was nowhere to go and no one to turn to. Veronica had been a good friend and someone that she had in her corner until that day when the paramedics came because her roommate had arrived from work and found her on the floor wearing those virtual reality headsets she worked on, a knocked over glass of wine on the carpet, and no pulse.

The EMTs said she had been killed instantly from the heart attack.

Best friend and confidante wiped in the blink of an eye.

Jakub's sister sounded really nice, much more genuine than the people she knew, but that was something she had always heard about people from Texas. Veronica was from Texas, too. She could use a new sister. Lindsey just felt so lost where she was now, everything was wrapped up in preserving the image and ego of someone else, someone that rarely paid attention to a damned thing she ever had to say.

Now she had some time to be alone, to be out miles away from home and watch people in their natural element. They seemed like an alien species, a weird strain of people that she wished she could be a part of. Couples that hugged each other when they got off the plane, people who shed tears of excitement, moved nervously with anticipation as the party they were waiting for arrived.

Nobody was waiting for her. Even the workmates that she would be working with didn't check to see if she made it or not, no one cared as long as she showed up at the convention center to haul boxes, unload things, and be the pack mule for the much more important and more highly paid sales teams.

Even the marketing girls didn't have too much to say to her. She'd had one special 'in' that helped get her in this gig, and that was only because the other marketing girl was pregnant and ready to drop any time now.

Part of her was jealous. She'd never know what that felt like, probably never have kids of her own, and that was a little nagging thing inside her, too. It's a natural woman thing, to become a mother. Maybe not everyone has that drive, but most do.

Lindsey did.

She had dreamed about it once. Beautiful little girl with light wavy hair. She looked like a little girl, but she talked like a little adult with a college degree. But then, dreams are like that.

She saw the couple across from her. Lindsey wasn't sure that they were necessarily a couple, the two girls seemed to be just more friendly than anything else, and they were seated a few aisles away facing her. One of them was a girl who had her head obscured mostly with a charcoal colored hoodie. She was wearing a pair of cargo shorts and Chucks. What caught Lindsey's eye was the purple butterfly tattooed on her shin.

It wasn't a common thing, and certainly something that was meant to be noticed as she sat in the hard plastic seat kicking her leg back and forth nervously.

The girl next to her was also in her mid 20s, long wavy coffee-colored hair and a big smile that was an eye-grabber as well. She was eyeing Lindsey for some reason she plainly couldn't determine. She lightly tapped the hoodie girl with a finger tipped in polish the color of a Cabernet and gestured. They both waved. Lindsey gave a polite smile and waved back, trying to figure out if she had ever seen them before.

Sometimes that happens, people see you and think they know who you are, obviously having mistaken you for someone else. If you're lucky, maybe it's someone famous. She had no idea why they might have thought they knew her.

Looking down at her phone, she was grateful that there were no new messages or texts. Lindsey didn't really care what Sarah was doing, as long as she wasn't bothering *her*.

When she looked back up, the girls were gone.

just can't see

It was the sound of water rushing that got Jakub's attention. It was thunderous, and the sky seemed bright, but he was in the shade. Then he realized it wasn't a he, but *they*. As he began to focus on his surroundings, Jakub understood that Hester and Shelaine were there with him.

They were seated on a huge log, one that was so large Jakub's feet barely touched the ground. The scene before him was spectacular, a pristine waterfall that looked like the long white hair of an old woman stringing into the cool pool of water before him.

Jakub looked up and saw they were underneath a palm tree.

Then he was scared.

"Am I dead?" He asked, looking at Hester. The question appeared to take him by surprise, then they laughed.

"No, sir. You're at the Millaa Millaa Waterfall in Queensland. That's Australia, by the way. It's about noon here." Hester seemed to remember he hadn't answered the question and continued, "We thought you might like a sight-seeing break. You're astral traveling in your sleep. We thought this might be a great place to come hang out, that's all."

"You always wanted to travel, right?" Shelaine asked, "What better way to start than this."

"Besides, we need to know you a little better if we're gonna look out for ya. Hanging out is just a good idea. What else are you gonna do in your sleep?"

"Oh, he'll find out soon enough," Shelaine said. "Let's make sure he has a break first."

"I don't think I understand," Jakub said. "I like it, I just don't understand."

"That's okay. We can get to that in a little bit. Right now, let's just relax. We got time."

Jakub surveyed Hester and Shelaine. They were dressed for the occasion, Hester's hat looking like something he'd seen on a golf course, one of those tan breezer hats. He just couldn't break the military thing, as he had on desert khaki cargo shorts and a pair of sandals.

Shelaine was dressed similarly, drab shorts with a lady's Hawaiian shirt. She noticed Jakub was surveying them and with a grin said, "Air Force deployment uniform. Seemed like a good time for it." Hester chuckled. Jakub knew there was a joke there, but he didn't get it. He also didn't ask.

"You're gonna start learning a lot of things very fast," Hester said. "Some of it's gonna bend your mind a little bit, but you can handle it. We're not really here for that."

"We're here for that a *little* bit," Shelaine said. "You have a date Saturday."

"I wouldn't call it a date," Jakub said, "I'm supposed to meet my therapist at a bar, but from the way she sounds, I highly doubt it's anything romantic."

"Oh, it's not romantic," Hester said, "And you're gonna find out she's more than a therapist, so you'll want to pay special attention to everything she's gonna teach you. This'll make more sense then, but you're gonna see a lot more of her. I mean more frequently, not *physically* more of her. Some other dude gets that gift."

"My god, Hess, can ya stop bein' a damn perv for just one minute?" Shelaine laughed, punching him.

"Nope."

Jakub was looking out at the rock, wet and slick, deep black from where the water had constantly saturated it. It flowed from the waterfall into a stream that sauntered off to their right, peaceful and serene. The temperature was moderate, and it was in the running for being the most perfect place on Earth. As the water rushed, it carried an energy with it, a wall of calm and fine mist that seemed to blanket him over and over, in time with every heartbeat.

Hester interrupted his thoughts again, "So, what was it about Veronica that hooked you. Besides her being a hottie, of course."

Jakub stopped to think. "It was probably the fact that she had the ability to know what I was really thinking and feeling. I mean, it was humiliating at first, cuz you know what a guy's mind is like. And the way she described it, the more emotional the thought, the more clear the thought was to her. Once we really began talking though, it felt almost like she was my right arm, and I don't think I'd ever had that level of communication with anyone else, like ever, y'know?"

"Communication does certainly prevent a lot of problems. They used to tell us all the time about the 6 Ps, and that certainly falls in there. If you talk, then you know what you're aiming at, where everyone is, and that makes things flow a lot better and succeed."

"6 Ps?"

"*Prior Planning Prevents Piss Poor Performance*," Shelaine answered, "It's pretty much a staple. Also why we're here talking to you. Last time you watched us all work, but you didn't really know what we were doing, why we were doing it, and it all seemed like a dream. But we're really here. All the time."

"Most of the time," Hester said, "What you do in your *really* private moments is your business, and we make sure we aren't around for that. So ya don't hafta feel all funny in the shower. I promise we've left the room to do other things."

"Have you ever considered being that way, having that closeness with anyone else? Is there anybody else you've wanted to have that level of trust with?"

"Not that I know would ever happen," Jakub said, "But yes, there's somebody."

"You haven't forgotten about her, have you?" Hester said knowingly.

Jakub exhaled abruptly. "No. And I've tried. But no."

"Maybe you shouldn't. I can't give too much away, but we'll just say there's a lot more to that story than you ever knew, and eventually it'll all come out. You're about to step into her world, where she's been living since she was a kid. So kinda take it easy on her. Both of you made some really stupid decisions instead of owning up to shit. It ain't gonna get fixed today, but I got a feeling that one day it will."

"When do I get to see Veronica again?"

"Ah, so ya remember that, do ya? I can tell you that she's still in her life Review, and we'll be there to pick her up when she gets out. We have our orders. But we also have a little time, so we're spending it here with you, like we're supposed to. After all, we're your advocates, not hers."

"So what exactly is this Review thing?"

"Welp, it's that thing that all those thumpers call the Judge-mint, where everybody's goin' to Hayul if they don't curry their weight 'round the compound and forfeit their spendin' cash to the Savior."

"Hester..." Shelaine warned.

"Ah. You're tryin' the Texas drawl. Nice. *Don't do that*. Takes a lot more practice," Jakub said to Hester, who laughed uproariously.

"Son, that's the best one you've come up with all day! I like that. But you get my drift. It's not that bad of a thing. You hafta account for all the crap you do in life, and believe me, there were some things I *didn't* want my Grandma hearin' about. Like that time with the two hookers off post in the Golden Sun Inn, and the Sergeant Major's wife I ran off with that time at the Stab n' Jab when I was still an E-4."

"That was *before* me," Shelaine clarified, "I don't want you getting the idea I'd actually put up with that crap on my watch."

"Still, it's basically where you go over your life, they have scenes in your life when you were supposed to go a certain way, and then you plainly went the wrong direction. But it's not anything like 'you bad dog', or anything like that. It's more like... you ever play sports in school?"

"No."

"But you know that in sports, you usually watch video of the other team before a game, so you can get a feel for how they play, the mistakes they make, what each player does that's specific to them?"

"I follow ya."

"It's like that, except you're kinda playin' against yourself. Looking at your own things. So there's not a lot of shame there, maybe a little embarrassment, but the few that are in the room with you are usually very supportive. It was pretty good for me, but the flip side is the fact that most of the shit you did the wrong way, you *knew* you were screwing up at the time. It was in your gut in the moment. I could have done something completely different with my life. It was going to go in another direction. But that mistake I don't take back. I'm happy to be who I am, and happy I ran into her. So for me, it was a bit of a wash. I think I got something better out of it, even if I had to go through a lotta bullshit to get there. I think you're gonna feel the same way when it's all said and done."

"What else do I have to look forward to?"

"Uhp... can't really go there, remember? All we can do is guide you through it when it comes. Little pointers and tips, some education along the way. We'll talk more about that after your date on Saturday. Then you'll have a better handle on things. Some lessons you just have to walk through yourself in order to learn 'em."

Shelaine perked up, "I'm more than likely going to deal with a lot of the women issues you have to deal with, because, well, I'm better equipped for that. You don't want Hester running that department, *trust me*."

"I'll handle more of the tactical side of things."

"There's a tactical side of things?" Jakub asked. He was feeling a twinge of apprehension.

"Well, yeah. You're not on a party boat. You're gonna learn harder truths than the average bear."

"What about the ranger, Yogi?" Shelaine led on playfully.

"*Fuck the ranger*, Boo-Boo!" Hester surveyed the area again. Jakub noticed that he had a habit of scanning everything on a repetitive basis, across, up, down. His eyes or his head were in almost constant movement.

"I noticed you never stop moving," Jakub said to Hester.

"Bad habit. Good habit, really, but you get it doing jobs like I did. You are always scanning for anything that moves or doesn't fit. It's a defense mechanism you learn as a grunt. Once you start, you're doing it every day for however many years, it doesn't let go of you. Been dead a decade, still looking for the shit that can't even hurt me anymore."

"Only time he stops is when he's asleep or meditating."

"*You* meditate?" Jakub asked, surprised.

"Well, yeah. Don't you? You hafta meditate. Keeps you from going crazy and your dong from shriveling like a cocktail weenie."

"I'm *not* sure about the cocktail weenie part," Shelaine said.

"Shhhh. I'm tryin' to properly train the young'un here. You *do* need to begin meditating, though. That's not negotiable. It helps you disconnect from your waking state in a way you'll need later. Calms and slows everything down. I wish I'd done it more when I was incarnate, but they didn't really push that shit for the jocky types at the time I was around. It was all 'big boys don't cry' and all that junk. Learn to meditate. Try not to start with a hot yoga teacher, or you'll never get anything done. You'll spend all day trying to discover the inner meaning of her yoga pants. And you'll be stuck dick first into the mat like a lawn dart. Trust me. There are better ways. Even if it might be a worthy thing to study."

"You sound like you have some experience with that," Shelaine said.

"Well, you know how they say when you're talking to a crowd, or sitting in a job interview, it's always easier if you just visualize them naked?"

"Yeah," she responded, eyeballing him.

"That's why I talk to *you* so much."

"Oh. My. Gawd," she huffed with a grin, punching him on his shoulder.

"Hey, it works. Now, back to the kid here. You haven't learned about vibrational levels and all of that yet, and I'll leave that to your mentor to hook you up on. But it's important too. Plays a big part in everything going on around ya. You *could* go study about it yourself, and I certainly wouldn't vote against it, but it's your call."

"The more you study what's available to you, the better off you'll be," Shelaine added.

"You'll have to wade through some streams of absolute horseshit, but the good news is that we can help clarify those things for you that ya have questions on since we're already here. You'll have a good idea on the level of crap you're about to enjoy based on the price they charge. We know of people that use every trick in the book, charge obnoxious amounts of money to fill you full of whatever they had to bullshit you with at the time. Your pocket's empty, your head's full of crap, and you're two steps backward in the game."

"If someone gives you a message and doesn't charge you a dime, and every point seems to check out, you might wanna investigate it. Chances are high that one of us is right there and can validate it for you. But we're gonna be really careful on who we let near you, so you have an advantage over most people."

"Like your momma," Shelaine said rather flatly, "Her advocate spends her time in a permanent facepalm, poor girl. Some people just don't get reality that well."

"So you know about all of that?" Jakub asked.

"Oh, yeah. She's a piece of work. We've went to great lengths to make sure you two are gonna be separated for a good, long while. Her level of garbage cramps my style, and I don't have time for her. Pretty sure you don't, either."

"Now that's some welcome news," Jakub said.

"Other advocates aren't allowed to mess with you either, unless we grant permission, and we grant permission with an eye on what you would want, or need. So if you're talking to another advocate, we gave the permission. Like Stanton, for instance. You might be working with his charge, but he ain't allowed within a country mile of ya."

"He'll probably try to find a way."

"And I'll stomp that pretty boy's ass like a fucking cockroach. I lose my good manners after a point. He knows better than to jerk with you or us. Speakin' of jerking, he's the kind of guy that would spy on his charge in the shower and then go spank his monkey like an angry zookeeper."

"Hess!" Shelaine hissed.

"I'm just sayin', if I hafta start something, The Lady'll finish it, and I *promise* he doesn't want any of that magic."

"Anything you particularly regret?" Jakub asked Hester.

'Well," he paused to think, "I can say you might want to avoid becoming close friends with anyone learning how to tattoo." He looked down as he extended his arms. "Not me, of course, all these were professional." He was especially surveying a dagger with a skull embedded hilt and topped with a Senior Jumpmaster Badge. On the two scrolls between the skull and badge, he saw they read STRIKE HOLD and BLUE DEVILS.

"Why's that?" Jakub inquired, "That looks pretty good to me."

"Oh, this... Three of us got this at the same time, off post at Bragg. 3rd of the 504th. They aren't around anymore. But no, once you help an amateur tattooist put 'Property of the US Navy' on the ass-cheek of a drunk and passed out cherry with an ego and an attitude, you've kinda made a commitment. I think that's all I wanna cop to about that. Hope he ain't a Sergeant Major now. Bet his wife gets a chuckle every night. Mine just beats on me."

no mercy to fear

Darcy left the message on Jakub's voicemail to meet her at the Tinder Statesman at 3:30 Saturday afternoon. She knew he had got the message because he came through the door three minutes early.

The entire bar had been decorated for what appeared to be a special event, Scottish flags on stringed banners around the room. They had placed tablecloths on all of the tables. Darcy hadn't seen those when she was there before.

"What's the big event, Stefan?" Jakub asked the bartender.

"Burn's Night. We're gonna keep the bar open at about 7:30 for regular patrons, but the rest of this is a per head deal. I think Fat Man charges about $80 a head. Bunch of assholes sitting around in skirts drinkin' Scotch and readin' poetry nobody gives a damn about."

"Kilts. They're called *kilts*, fuckhead," Mack boomed, emerging from the back. "And yeah, it's a big deal. And yes, lotsa people give a damn about Robbie Burns. Hafta pay a pretty penny for it every year, but it's an event I know will always be attended. Profit margin ain't huge, but it's worth it. Have most of it catered. But they know what they're doing. So, are you guys in?"

Mack appeared to be very proud of himself.

"We have a genuine haggis and everything. One of the best nights of the year. I gotta keep the MacGregors happy."

"Certainly a night I'll be at home. I'm not a Scot. I'd be pretty outta place," Jakub said.

"Certainly a night I'll be using my wireless ear buds so I don't hafta listen to that shit all night," Stefan said to Jakub. Fat Man grunted and gathered up a few loose papers on the bar, then headed to the back.

Jakub scanned for Darcy and headed to her table in the corner. They were chit-chatting, and Darcy hadn't yet brought up the real reason they were there when something abnormal caught her attention.

The smile caught her eye. It was the kind that could light up a room, and it was on the face of a young college-aged girl that had her eyes on Jakub, watching his every move. She was slightly hunched over, twirling a strand of wavy dark brown hair between her fingers. She looked Latina, but that was common in Texas. The dress she was wearing, a bright pink flowery print, made her look like she'd walked out of the pages of a magazine. As Jakub caught a slight sight of her and began turning his head, Darcy watched her completely vanish.

A moment later she reappeared, two tables away to the left. Darcy hadn't seen her move. She still had the wicked smile on her face as she watched Jakub. It all seemed a bit creepy. As her eyes locked with the girl, the young woman pointed at Jakub and made a sweeping motion with her fingers. There was something about her eyes that just seemed to take you over.

She wants me to send him away. I wonder what this is about? Probably gonna ask for his number.

"Jakub, could you be a dear and pick me up a diet coke and some fries? Have him put a lime in it, too. And get whatever you want." She could see the girl still sitting, slightly cocked back on the seat waiting for him to exit and still smiling.

Jakub got up and rounded the corner out of sight, which allowed Darcy to devote her full attention to the mystery woman who surprised her by completely vanishing again into thin air and Darcy felt herself jolt when the girl reappeared on the seat next to her. It felt like the air conditioner had been turned on and aimed right at her.

"So he's out of the way for a few minutes," the girl said happily, "I'm actually here for him, but I know I need to talk to you first, so here I am."

"Why do you need to talk to me?" Darcy asked her.

"You can see me. He can't... yet. But he'll be able to soon. He's developing pretty quickly. I think you're doing a great job with him. While we're on the subject of seeing people, do you see a fellow over at that table near the window? Blue blazer? Armani, probably."

"No."

The girl appeared confused. "Well how about that?" She mused.

"Do you need to cross over, too?"

The girl snorted, "Naw, sweetie, I'm not a customer, I'm upper management. I came in to poke around a little bit. I assume you're here for Garry. That poor bastard needs to *go*. This is probably the worst place you could be stuck. Dunno why he decided to light here, but maybe he doesn't know as much about this junk as I do. The last place on Earth you wanna be stuck at is in a bar. Alcohol lowers the vibration, so nobody here's gonna see him, much less let him find a way to cross over. It's like beating your head against a wall just to see if it hurts."

"Yes, we're here for Garry. Do you know him?"

"Nah, like I said, I'm here just to check on my boy there. I like Jakub. I already know why she's so ga-ga over him. He's a cutie, that's for sure. Not like he really has a choice. Damned good genes. If I didn't know the backstory on him or the black rabbit, I'd think him a little odd, though. Real problem is, he's lighting up like a searchlight. That wasn't supposed to happen this time. Pretty soon, every dead person in a mile radius is gonna be following him around like a pack of lost puppies, and I don't know he's ready for that yet. But you'll get 'im all straightened out, I'm sure. You'll want to do a real good job of it. You never know, he might be your boss one day. And of course, you could be selfish about it because there are awesome things headed your way." She paused to give Darcy a mischievous grin, "*Really* awesome things. After all, you can't grieve forever, right? You have to become a merry widow at some point. Just don't be afraid of it when it happens. Go with it. You'll know when it's right."

As Darcy felt the shock hit her, the girl vanished again. No one knew about Clayton, her late husband, not around here, anyway. Most people just assumed she was divorced, and she never bothered to correct them. It made things easier because it allowed her to play somewhere in her mind like he was still alive out there somewhere, far away from her voluntarily, and that gave her a temporary *get out of pain free* card to play over and over again as she saw fit.

Then again, there were positives in him being dead.

She was so good at helping other people with their problems, but when it came to her own, that was a minefield she'd just rather not walk around in. And this girl, whoever she was, not only knew about it, but pretty much threw an old burning tire right into the middle of it.

Darcy liked keeping everyone on a need-to-know basis. She couldn't explain or defend her actions, but they felt necessary. Like alienating the entire Stanton family after her husband's death, moving across the country, keeping her house devoid of personal markings to the point of sterility. It was something that she felt had to be done.

The only visitors she had to her home were business, and it had been two years since another human had seen the inside of her bedroom.

She wondered who the girl was with the dress. Something about her had felt so calm, yet so immensely powerful. She had smelled of lavender.

Jakub saw Garry enter the bar, look around as if he was looking for someone. Apparently he *was* looking for someone.

Jakub.

He walked right up to the table Darcy and Jakub were sitting and moved into the seat between them. He took an extended look at Darcy as if he were examining a statue.

"What's goin' on, Garry?" Jakub greeted him.

"I'm done drinkin'," Garry said, "Tell that nice lady with ya that I wanna go home now."

"Where's home?" Jakub asked him.

"Anywhere but here. But I wanna go. Don't leave me here."

"I can hear you, Garry," Darcy said, shifting to face him. "And I'm not gonna leave you, I promise. Sounds like you're ready. We can help you with that, but I need you to listen to me real close, okay?"

"Whatever you say, boss lady. Just get me the hell outta here."

She turned to Jakub. "When you look at Garry, what do you see?"

"Garry. Why? Just a normal guy."

"But, honey," Darcy said, "That's just it. Garry's *not* a normal guy. He's dead. He's passed, but he hasn't crossed over."

Jakub took a moment to process it. So *that's* why he always feels so cold when you're around him, why he never drinks his drinks, and Stefan can't hear him. Like Veronica was.

"You've become a physical medium. That's someone that can see the dead as well as they can see the living. One of the ways you can tell the difference is when they feel like you're walking next to a block of ice. Remember telling me about that?"

"Mmhmm."

"Notice how the temperature dropped when he pulled up a chair and sat down?"

"Yeah."

"Nobody else here saw him sit down. They don't see him here now." She scanned the room with her eyes and continued, "They assume I kicked the chair back with my foot, nobody knows he pulled the chair back himself. And that's another sign someone has been stuck for a while. Being able to move things takes time to figure out and get the power to do."

Darcy looked at Garry for a moment and said, "That's why he goes outside, isn't it Garry? You pick up energy from the people on the street because they have higher vibrational patterns. Less alcohol means stronger energy."

Garry looked down at the table, almost as if ashamed.

"It's alright, Garry," Darcy soothed, "You have to do what you have to do. Nobody's faulting you. Do you know how long you've been here?"

"No."

"You've been here almost seven years. But that's ending today. You're gonna get some peace and a new start. Everything you dealt with here will be finished. It'll be over. It all gets better after this."

She turned to Jakub and said, "I should probably show you something that will be useful in the future. Garry, sorry about this. Gotta do it." She took her hand and looked like she was going to slap him in the chest, but her hand flowed smoothly through him, the facade of what was Garry swirling like a column of wispy smoke that then re-formed.

"My god," Jakub said, feeling the shock in the pit of his stomach. Garry really had been an illusion of sorts all this time!

"So Garry, let me explain what we're gonna do. You're going to see a door. I don't know where it's going to form just yet, but when you see it, we're going to open it. You're going to see a bright light coming from that door, like really white. It'll be like someone was shining one of those airline spotlights in your face. I want you to walk into it. You should see someone you recognize when you step up to it. Start walking, keep going. That's all you have to do. You have the easy part." Darcy turned to Jakub and said, "You've done something like this before. So let's get it done."

She reached out her hands to Jakub and said, "Take my hands. Same thing you did with Jeanette. Find a position to relax, and breathe in." He could tell that she was gauging his body responses and said, "Good. Now I want you to imagine spikes coming out of your feet, like tree roots, sinking down into the ground. Just feel them out until they stop."

"Okay."

"Now, we are going to picture a door. It can be any design, any look you want. Something that is comfortable or familiar to you. Whatever you see in your mind's eye works. This isn't a high-tech adventure." She paused for a moment, breathing in.

It felt like they were completely disconnecting from the world around them, and he couldn't hear the ambient noise of the room anymore. It was just him, Darcy, and Garry standing there nervously. Jakub realized that although they were sitting down, it felt as if the three of them were standing up, the door appearing behind Garry, off to Jakub's right.

"Jakub, I want you to direct your energy to the door. Feel it well up in you, and when it starts feeling hot and thick, maybe a little more elastic, push it towards the door."

They breathed for a few more breaths.

"Open the door. Just reach out and pull it towards you."

Jakub took a moment to examine it before he opened it. The door was familiar, like the front door they had when he was growing up in La Grange. It was a special door, because he had helped his father go pick it up from the woodworkers' shop. They had brought it home, the sweet smell of the wood hanging in his nostrils like a manly perfume. Dad had shown him for the first time how to set hinges, how to use a wood chisel. Taught him how to set and install the door latch and jamb. It was ornate, and Dad was so proud of that door. Jakub had been so proud of it, too. And that was the door he was looking at behind Garry.

The tension was growing, it was thick, pensive, like those moments when you're scared to death of something but have to go through it anyway.

"Don't be afraid, Garry. I can feel it in you. This isn't gonna hurt," Darcy said, "I want you to turn around and look." Jakub watched as Garry turned his head first, and upon recognizing the door, swung his whole body around. It appeared he was having difficulty believing what he was seeing.

"Let's open this door," Darcy said, "Just reach out and pull it open." The light was peeking around the edges, and as Jakub pulled it open, he felt as if he needed sunshades. He heard Garry gasp. "It's okay, Garry. There's nothing to be afraid of."

Jakub saw a figure emerging from the light, appearing to be about four feet tall. It was a little girl with curly, disheveled copper hair. She was holding an equally fuzzy teddy bear in one hand, arm under the bear's arm, wrapped crosswise around its neck.

She looked up at Garry, who was beginning to quiver and shake. She grinned a bright grin with a missing upper tooth. "Come on, Daddy!" She said, reaching her other hand up.

He paused.

"It's your time to go with her, Garry. She's here for *you*."

"Come *on*, Daddy!" The girl repeated.

Garry reached forward and took her hand. The little girl pulled and began walking back into the light. Garry disappeared with her.

Jakub felt as if a switch had been flipped, the tension in the air dissipated immediately into a calm, crisp ambience.

And then the yelling.

He heard it over his shoulder, a loud and anxious, "Hold that door, motherfucker!"

They could feel it was feminine, but was moving so fast he couldn't track it as it zipped into the door like an arrow.

"Well, now," Darcy said, "You get those from time to time. Just let 'em through. You want everyone that will go through to get through."

She waited a moment. "Anybody else?" The room still felt calm. Then satisfied they were finished, she said to Jakub, "Okay, push that door closed and seal the edges with your hand, like you were coating it in gel or something. You have to close these things out when you finish with them."

Jakub reached out and followed Darcy's instructions as the light dissipated.

"Okay, now we're gonna take a minute to calm back down and get things in order." After a few breaths, she said, "Open your eyes."

It was like looking into a new world for the first time as the light burned his eyes from the room. It had been as if they were in an alternate reality.

"You're going to be tired after these things. I would suggest going straight home and taking a nap. You'll probably need to eat something. We'll catch up in a few days. Your training has now officially begun, and you can thank Jeanette Falkner for that. She was pretty adamant that I mentor you. Don't know what she might have told you."

Darcy was right. He felt as if he was a tire, and someone had let the air out.

closer to true

The crew Lindsey was going to be part of arrived at the convention center while it was still dark outside. There was a lot of work to do before the floor opened and the various attendees made their rounds looking to collect all the free stuff they could carry.

She checked in with a brunette girl named Jennifer that had her set up the folding tables for their booth, lay out the tablecloths with the company logo, and then directed her to meticulously line up all of the articles on the table as if she were a drill sergeant at boot camp.

It was really a small price to pay for the free trip. Sure, there were some things she had to cover, like meals, for the most part, and the last day that she was staying behind, but she had a little freedom, the nights were hers, and there were other things to be accomplished. All she really had to do was keep track of trinkets for two days and all was well.

She had been invited to dinner the first night, and that had been incredibly civil, all on the dime of the company, which was a nice switch. Her co-workers were friendly, even Jennifer, but she stayed away from personal information, as she always did, and made sure to deflect all of those sorts of questions back onto the others she was with, patiently listening as she was filled with information she didn't really need to know, but had to fake it to pay for her spot and possibly ensure having this as a backup plan some other time.

Two gentlemen dressed somewhat for business, more for the conference strolled by, then stopped. They looked at the tables, then looked at her and her colleagues.

The two young men chatted briefly as the more casual looking of the two cast an eye towards Lindsey. He nodded to the other man and seemed to usher him towards her co-workers, who were more than happy to occupy the gentleman at the other end of the table.

Here we go.

He approached cautiously and gently said to her, "I know this is gonna sound strange, and I swear I'm not trying to hit on you. But I think you're gonna understand what I'm about to say." He paused for a moment, took another good look at her and continued, "There's a girl right behind you, shaved red hair, yellow blouse. She knows I can see her, and most other people can't. She keeps doing this strange thing where she points at you, then she makes this 'call me' signal, like this," he said, using his thumb and pinky to resemble a phone.

The man looked quizzically just past her, then glanced around to see if anyone was watching. "She has this other thing. She points at herself, then she points at the chair. If this helps, she has a tattoo of a lotus on her right wrist, right here."

Lindsey actually saw him blush. "I'm really sorry, I don't do this much in public, and it's not a habit I make to talk to young women about people nobody can see, it's just a thing I have. My wife could tell ya if she was here. She has these... abilities, too."

"You're mediums."

"Excuse me?"

"You and your wife are mediums. I'm familiar. It runs in my family. Mother's side. I saw that girl in the airport. She might not have the hoop earrings in, but she was with a taller Latina yesterday." He nodded.

"I don't see that one. And now with the chair thing again. My name's Rector. Rector Williamson." He shook his head, "And no, I don't know why my parents named me that. I think they've forgotten why, but the joke's on me."

Rector still wasn't completely focused on Lindsey, but whoever was behind her. The intensity continued to build in his face until he finally blurted out, perhaps a little too loudly, "Are you her guide? Yes. The chair. I don't know what you're talking about with the chair. C name. Chair? Claire? Clarisse? No." He looked again at Lindsey, "I don't know. She's your guide. Has a name that starts with a 'C'. Has an abnormal obsession with a chair, chairs, *your* chair, something. I'm sorry, that's the best I can do. I'll leave ya alone now."

"No, wait..." She heard herself say.

He turned around to look at her, that deer in the headlights look that is of a fear of being recognized. She knew the look well. "*Thank you*," she said softly.

"Don't mention it. It was my honor. I hope it makes more sense at some point." He lightly nodded, no sense of anything on his face, nervous yet vacant.

It was reassuring to know that there was someone looking out after her, even if she didn't know who they were. Jeanette knew all about that stuff, she didn't. Maybe she would ask when she got back home, if she could remember to. And if Sarah would take her thumb off her neck long enough.

Nights alone in the hotel were almost pure solace. She figured Sarah was probably off chasing some ass while she was gone. It wasn't like her patterns had escaped Lindsey. She'd been played from the word go, and although she knew it deep in her heart, she still felt the need to defend it, ignore it, act like it wasn't the creeping thing that it was.

But the fact was, Lindsey was beginning not to care anymore. This driving for this goal, this purpose she now had held many facets in it that only made sense to her. They only unfolded in her mind, deep where she wouldn't let them be seen or known by anyone else.

She began with the television, but there was nothing that she could particularly seem to enjoy or even find an interest in. Lindsey could take long baths without interruption, and they had a trance-trip-hop channel that seemed to put her right where she wanted to go.

In this hotel room, she was alone, but she wasn't lonely. It was almost peace.

Almost.

too much to think

They were smoking cigarettes on the back deck, nippy for the time of year. You know the people that really care about their smoking, because they'll be the ones outside braving cold and rain for a drag of tobacco. This was the place they came to vegetate for brief moments and pretend sometimes that they were getting their allowance of vitamin K for the day.

"What if I told you some really wild shit's starting to happen to me?" Jakub asked. It looked like the sentence was something he'd thought out and carefully constructed.

"Define '*wild shit*'."

"Recently I found out that I see dead people." He said it like it was a mic drop.

"Okay. Some people do that. I'm cool with that. Doesn't change how I think of you, if that was what you were worried about. I've been looking at some interesting stuff myself."

"Yeah?"

"Yeah. Energy healing. I met this girl when I was in Colorado that does it. I mean, I'd heard of it, just like I've heard of mediums and tarot card readers.

You have a lot that are full of crap, but the ones I've seen that are the real deal are all a lot like you, just real quiet and genuine folk. I guess that might be why it doesn't surprise me much. Anyway, I watched girl work, and had her do a session on me. Hafta admit, she was *really* cute. But she was more interested in doing the job than interested in me, so that was good. Had a day where I was a little loose on the backside, but it was about like a day after a chiropractor. I don't even think she laid a hand on me. No matter how much I wanted her to."

"So it worked for you?"

"Yeah, I'm thinking about learnin' how to do that stuff. She says anyone can learn to do it. Might as well test that notion. But enough of my weirdness, I wanna hear about what you've been seeing. Tell me about dead folks!"

"It started, well at least I *think* it started with a guy I kept seeing at the bar. It was this fella named Garry. I just thought he looked a little rough and had a bad day. Then it crossed my mind he was dead. Okay, so that's bullshit. I had no freakin' clue. By the time Darcy got in the picture, I discovered he *was* actually a dead guy. I didn't realize there was anything after this. I mean, after the whole thing with Veronica, I still had my reservations, y'know, maybe that was just some wild extended dream or something. There have been times when I thought I was just out of my mind on that whole deal. But here's this guy, and she can see and talk to him, too."

Aiden just listened intently and let him talk. It struck him that this might be the actual first time he'd talked about it outside therapy, so he let him just go.

"Then the dreams started. Like there are these people that are actually in charge of helping our lives go the way they're supposed to go. That thought never crossed my mind before, that I might actually have help in life, that there was an actual plan for things that was out there, and I couldn't see it. I was just living it blind, but not really. It's kinda neat and scary at the same time."

"You mean like guides?" Aiden offered.

"Yeah, they've talked about that. But they call them advocates. They say that we call them guides, but that's not the technical term that they call themselves. I mean, here's the mind job... so in this dream I had, I was taken to this hotel in Serbia, and you know me, I've never left the country in my life. We actually had some sort of weird meeting there, and I met several of these people. I wake up, and a day or two later I'm thinking about the dream, so I go look up this hotel, and it actually exists! I went to the website, and everything, including the restaurant we were in are *actually there*, like I could hop a plane now and go sit in the seat I was in during the dream!"

"Now *that* is cool. It's sounding to me like you're in the beginning of something that's gonna be really special. Have you got beyond the part where you doubt yourself, then? I know that I've heard of stuff like this before, and I know that you're not alone. There are entire communities of people that experience paranormal things directly. I think I might have a person or two to talk to if you ever wanna. From what I've heard, it's somewhat related to the things I'm getting interested in."

"So tell me a little about this whole energy thing. If they're related, I probably need to learn more about it, because I'm the first to admit I'm an absolute novice at all this."

"Well, I am too, to be perfectly honest. But I watched this girl relieve headaches, stop joint pains, all kinds of stuff. I mean whatever she did to me, it worked. She told me about this other guy that keeps himself pretty hid away, but he does this stuff remotely." Aiden paused, "Yeah, I'm serious. I thought it was a bit of bullshit myself. Apparently she knows at least three cases personally where he's done this intercontinentally. He actually helped reduce an ovarian cyst in Europe from his apartment. None of them want to take credit for any of it, though. They say that this energy runs through them, like a conduit, and they simply direct it where it needs to work, and the energy does the rest."

"That's trippy."

"Yeah. I'm still on the fence with it. I wanted to look into it and see what else I could find before I just accept the idea blindly, so I'm tellin' ya the little I know. You'll hafta research it on your own. But I'm beginning to think that there's more to life that I thought was there, I'm telling ya that much. Means that I ain't even close to exploring the sheer amount of area I could."

"You're really soaking up the Texas thing."

He couldn't help but chuckle. "Why do ya say that?"

"You've adopted the word 'ain't' like long-lost kin. The drawl is startin' to sink in. You remember when you first got here, everybody asked you where you were from?"

"Yeah."

"Notice nobody does that anymore?"

He thought about it. It was true. No one asked him where he was from anymore. Everyone assumed he was from Texas. It was now only when he left the state people asked where he was from.

"Yeah, the guy at the soda brewery asked me if I was from Texas. I was really proud of myself."

Jakub tapped his fingertips against each other, and in the most crookedly evil voice he cackled, "Your transformation is *almost* complete."

Aiden snorted, "Then what's the last part?"

"Lone Stars. I swear to God you'll end up with one somewhere, or end up wearing one. It's unavoidable. We can't stop ourselves. You notice it's like on every single building you see. I mean, California was beautiful and special, don't get me wrong, but there is just something intrinsically different here. The people are different, everything is like its own world."

"Yeah, I have to admit I had my doubts when I first started spending time here. It's different visiting than it is making it your home. I think that the other things we're looking at are the same way. Once you're in that world, you just suck it up, breathe it in, and become part of it. I'm gonna do a little reading and see what it feels like to me. I can always call up girl up north if I have any questions, but my gut feels good about it. I think I might pursue it."

"You probably should. I mean. If you feel a pull to it, I've learned that there is usually a good reason for it, and maybe we shouldn't fight against them."

"She's really cute. I'm gonna hafta go to someone else for that stuff. I don't think I'd be able to concentrate."

"Then go to someone else. Find some crusty dude that looked like he crawled out of a mesquite bush."

Aiden laughed, "I just got a visual of that. It'd be like the shaggy guy from Monty Python that was always popping up everywhere. Not the first guy you wanna claim was your teacher."

"Exactly."

"What about your mentor? I haven't met her yet. Just heard about her."

"She's pretty, I guess. You know she fills multiple roles for me, so I can't even think like that. It'd be both wrong and illegal. Unethical, anyway. I'm the sick patient in need of healing, remember?"

"Sounded to me that she's not healing you of anything anymore. You're more like her padawan now."

"Well, since ya put it that way, yeah. I guess you could call it that. Same rules apply."

"Of course. Do ya get to pay her off in brisket?"

"I don't think so. I think that's just Ms. Echols."

"Doesn't sound to me like you're castin' a wide enough net. Amazing what can be accomplished with a good meal."

"Which reminds me. Willie wants us to bring the torture water next weekend. They're cooking."

"Count me in. I ain't stupid. I know a good meal when I hear about it. What does Carl need fixin' this time?"

"Nothin', I don't reckon. It was just a case of Willie deflecting me givin' her a hard time."

"Then we should probably do that more often. I don't mind getting a free meal out of it."

"You know," Jakub said, eyeing him, "There's no such thing as a free lunch."

"Matter of perspective."

"Matter of economics."

"My stomach is a gas tank, not a calculator. It does empty, and it does full. It doesn't like averages."

"She said somebody called her wanting to talk to her instead of me, or called her about me, something. She won't say what it has to do with. I tried to get it out of her. Wouldn't budge."

"Probably got a girl stalkin' ya."

"I doubt that. Girls don't stalk me." Jakub paused, "Oh, wait. I guess at least one has, now that I think about it. I didn't think about it being a girl, I figured it was a bill collector or something."

"Because we wouldn't want to get your hopes up or anything..."

"Exactly."

"Why would it be a bill collector? What do you owe?"

"Nothin' I can think of. I just needed an idea to work with. You never know. I can't think of who would be that interested in what I'm doing. She says she thinks it's a good thing, though."

"It's a girl. She's gonna marry you off to the highest bidder. Try to get a cow or somethin' for ya."

"That's not how a dowry works. You pay the dad for the daughter."

"Anything's possible in Texas. Had a guy I met once tell me that when he was overseas, his squad leader had an offer put in on him by a sheik. I think it was a camel and three Arabian horses. They had to tell the man they couldn't trade soldiers. He only wanted one night. I think you're selling yourself short with just a cow, to be honest. At least demand a Longhorn steer, maybe a couple pigs thrown in."

"Nobody's tradin' livestock for me. They wouldn't have the room, anyway."

"So I guess we haven't ruled out the possibility then."

"You better watch it. I'll have her sell you off to some waitress at a diner. One that has less teeth than she has kids."

"As long as she trades in pairs. Somebody needs to get enjoyment, maybe some sexual healing outta this transaction."

Jakub snorted, "You'd actually go along with this whole horse-trading thing?"

"Oh, hell no. I'm just bullshittin'. You want the Black Cherry next, or the Birch Beer?"

natural

Willie watched the rental pull up outside the diner, and it just felt right, like she already knew who was going to get out of the car before they did.

In a single second, she understood why Jakub had spent three solid years whining about the girl. Lindsey, with her close crop and dyed streak was still so beautiful it hurt. Mom would have been on her like a piranha on a diver's leg.

She looked sad, even when she smiled.

They took a few moments to introduce themselves and get seated.

"There comes a time when ya have to weigh out how much you're going to hurt someone to get what you want for yourself," Lindsey said, tracing the ridge of her coffee cup with the tip of her finger. It seemed like there was so much she wanted to blurt out, but was forcibly stopping herself. "I'm really not that person, never have been. Whatever window I might have ever had is lost. He's in love with Veronica, and she is plainly still in existence, and very much in love with him. We were about as much like sisters as you could get without biology. That becomes sacred ground, and I'm not enough of a bitch to cross it. So I'm doing the next best thing and trying to amplify anything good I can recover from it, for both of their sakes."

They sat quietly for a moment. It was plain to see that Lindsey was uncomfortable for a reason she hadn't yet admitted to.

"Oh, screw it," she finally said. "You remember when I called that time and I said that I had interference?"

"Yeah. I wondered what that was about, but I am guessing your partner?"

"That would be the one."

"So how did that come about?"

"What, the call?"

"No, the partnership, relationship, whatever."

She exhaled and took a sip of her coffee.

"I don't know what the hell I'm doing. But this is how it happened. I used to be a courier, y'know, a person that delivers packages and documents quickly in the city. We were used a lot in the legal and entertainment fields to get things moved all over the city like yesterday. We were very time-critical as a business. I needed the workout. I needed the anonymity."

She paused, and it seemed like she was trying to gather courage to continue.

"So I saw your brother when he was working at McTannis & Kitcher with Sarah." She smiled and shook her head, looking embarrassed, "Oh my god, I was *all* about him. I would stalk him relentlessly, I knew when he got to work, when he went to lunch, I even tried to run into him a few times, but it was like he just didn't see me. I know his middle name, even."

"No you don't. I think there are less than ten people on Earth that know his middle name. He leaves it off everything, and we have no idea where he got it anyway."

"Xander. With an 'X'. Jakub Xander Riser."

She felt her jaw drop. "How the hell do you know that?"

"I told you I was *all* about him."

Lindsey was blushing. It was cute. Willie couldn't remember ever seeing a girl blush over her brother before, including the ones, he'd brought home from California. Knowing what she'd meant to Jakub just made it an even sweeter thing to witness.

Her face fell. "I know I'm not much to look at, but I figured that maybe I'd get lucky, and he'd at least say something to me. He was really friendly the first time I saw him, and then he just gave me the cold shoulder after that. Maybe I shouldn't have tried to give him my phone number. Maybe *that* was it."

"Wait, what?" Willie was incredulous. "Say that again. You did what?"

"I wrote my number down on a piece of paper, and I gave it to Sarah to give to him."

Willie couldn't help but grin. She knew exactly where this was going, but she wanted to see just how bad it had gone.

"That might have been your first mistake."

"Didn't sound like it. Not from what he said about me."

"Did you hear it from his mouth?"

"No."

"Then it wasn't said. Trust me. But what did *she* say he said?"

"That I wasn't his type of girl. Talking shit about how fucked up he thought my body was. And that I was too crazy and damaged for him anyway." She looked crushed.

"Did I just hear that right?"

"I believe so."

"And that's what you've been carrying around all this time. I bet I know the next move on this one. Next you started hearing how beautiful you were, how nobody has the right to say things like that, and he's a prick, but he has a good heart so you shouldn't hate him too much."

"Basically. How did you know?"

"My mother is a champion at that. And it's all bullshit. I can sit here with 110% authority and tell you that those words, nor remotely anything like them have ever escaped the lips of my brother. Ever. Not on this planet, or any other. She might be your girlfriend, but that bitch needs to be throat-punched."

Lindsey seemed to recoil a bit, confused. That was okay. The girl would need some time to realize exactly how far she'd been manipulated, and this might actually be the first thing she had done of her own volition in quite some time.

The funny thing about her was that no matter what state she was in, the girl just seemed to light up naturally with her own little glow that made you like her before she opened her mouth or even had any interaction with you.

"But enough with threatening your girlfriend. What was it that you actually wanted to talk about?" She saw that she'd shaken the poor girl up a little bit, so she went again with a different question. "Tell me about the rabbit. What's that about?"

Lindsey lit up.

"So, you know all about Veronica, and how she had passed, but her spirit, essence, whatever you wanna call it was still stuck in the VR headset, right?"

"With ya so far."

"Well, she was actually able to use the device the same way Jakub could because she was still at a low level of electricity. As bizarre as it sounds, she had the same relative electrical impulse as the pointer Jakub used. So she got into her shopping account from a few years ago when she was alive, and since she still had a gift card on the account, she bought the rabbit and had it shipped to his house!" Lindsey was giggling with glee, "Can you just imagine? It had to be the first time the Internet has ever been used by the dead to send gifts!"

"You're serious." She wasn't quite sure she believed this crap.

"Yes," she nodded. "That's why it goes with him everywhere. She actually sent it to him in a package. Somehow everyone had turned all her accounts off except that one, and if she hadn't had the gift balance still in there, it wouldn't have happened. So gift card balances are a good thing. Especially if you ever find yourself trapped in a pair of VR goggles."

"I frequently do. But not for that reason," Willie replied, "Have you ever actually used VR yourself?"

"No, can't say I ever got the opportunity. I hear it's really cool, though."

"You have no idea. We're gonna hafta spoil ya and break ya in one of these days." She shook her head and decided to just go there.

"That whole thing about 'I'm not much to look at'? You can drop the modesty with me." Lindsey looked genuinely confused. "You're serious. That's what you actually believe?"

"Well, yeah." She watched her shoulders pull in tighter. Abuse. This girl was going through emotional abuse.

I am so fucking that girl up when she gets in my range, Willie thought, *I'm smashing her world like an armadillo in the goddamned road.*

"You look like you walked out of a television set, or off the cover of a magazine. You're naturally and *exquisitely* beautiful. You can't hide that shit. The fact that you can't see it yourself's irking me to no end, because that tells me somebody's been very fucked to you, and nothing, I mean *nothing* on Earth pisses me off more than people being fucked with when they aren't in a position to defend themselves." She paused, and the flash clicked in her head. "You got bullied when you were a kid, didn't you?" She seemed to blush and cower a bit.

"Yes. It didn't stop until I left high school."

"My fucking god. *Now* this bullshit makes sense." She did the only thing she could think of in the moment. She got up, went to the other side of the booth and wrapped her arms around her, pulling her close.

Lindsey apparently did the only thing she could think of in the moment.

She let go.

The girl cried. Hard.

Now was not the time to bring out the fact that Jakub had been so head over heels for her it was almost disgusting. Now was time to deal with the badly broken girl he didn't have any idea he was so in love with.

"My mother taught me how to deal with bullies," Willie said. "Not because she didn't like them, but because she *is* one. We're always in a state of active war with her. You haven't been able to have the conversations you should have had from the start with Jakub, or you'd have been so unfortunate to have heard about it. But I'm in your corner now.

You need anything, you call us. And I mean *anything*."

She nodded and tried to clean up her face with napkins.

Lindsey had never let that out before, not to anyone she'd just met, especially. It seemed like Willie had so much momma in her that she brought love and security and laid it on the table like that night's dinner. Some things didn't really lure Lindsey in, but that had. And she felt a sense of trust that she wasn't completely familiar with.

Knowing that you aren't the most typical girl in the world is one thing. Having someone there that made it a point to treat you as if you were the most normal thing to blue in the sky was another experience.

She thought about the reasons she'd actually begun stalking Jakub in the first place, the things she'd noticed about him from day to day. He seemed gentle to everyone. In the winter, he'd leave his car unlocked so a couple of the homeless could get change out of his cigarette ashtray. He'd even tell them it was there. Had covered for them at least once that she knew of.

He didn't drink back then. Not that she knew of. He felt right to her, like a storybook prince that had been hiding himself away for just the right moment to let everyone know he was the benevolent ruler of the world or something.

She had tried to get into the same elevators as he did. Found out where he was and tried to get packages that were meant for his floor. She even lied about the packages she had a couple of times, but she couldn't get close enough.

Until one day. He had looked into her eyes, and she felt the earth move like an earthquake. She wanted to speak. She didn't know if he wanted to speak, too, or if he was just sick.

That was the day she met Sarah.

Lindsey had tried to buddy up to Sarah, get in close in hopes of getting to him. She had seen them talking, figured they were friends. They never went anywhere together, so it couldn't be more than that.

Veronica had listened to her each night after work, when she wasn't busy, but then again, Veronica would stop anything she was doing to talk to Lindsey. They were like two peas in a pod, sisters from a different mister, and she hadn't had that level of friendship before in her life.

She still couldn't muster the confidence to ever tell Veronica his name, to speak it aloud.

Lindsey tried to get Sarah to give him her phone number, or at least get his for her. The next day was when she dashed all of Lindsey's hopes around her ears. What she'd told Lindsey he said about her tore her into little pieces and completely dismantled her. That failed experiment had dashed her hopes of ever being normal.

Soon Jakub was gone.

She knew his middle name. Very few people did. But he was her love and obsession from afar, and now there was little else.

Veronica tried what she could to argue the case, but not knowing who she was arguing for, it quickly went to nothing. Next thing Lindsey knew, she was being seduced.

By Sarah.

It was a slippery slope from there. And then when Jakub was around again, she was afraid to be alone with someone that had despised her so much, and Sarah wouldn't let that happen anyway.

It did strike her odd that with what had been said, Sarah would still take time to hang out with him like nothing ever happened. But she was a strange creature herself. A very pretty creature, still strange.

At the hotel, she prepared for her last night before the early morning flight. Everything had been packed and was ready to go, to a place that wasn't feeling like home anymore, like she was on work release, and now she had to go back and hole up in the metal soup can again.

She looked at herself again in the bright bathroom lights, tried to survey herself to understand what it was these people all thought they saw.

I look like an elf.

For the first time, she stopped to think about what had just crossed her mind. Her face was thin, but not abnormal, her green eyes shone in the lights of the vanity, and with her blonde hair, even with the dyed streak, she could be an elf. Like a from-the-movies elf. They *were* pretty.

I could totally do battle armor. Or one of those badass Galadriel dresses.

He had talked to his sister about *her*. "He speaks very highly of you," she'd said. That didn't sound like a guy that thought she was disgusting. You wouldn't mention it again if you saw someone you weren't attracted to. It would be like looking at a subway wall, you don't go home to your mother and tell her all about it.

Then the feeling as she surveyed herself in the mirror to finally declare anything worth looking at, and realized she had the hairs on the back of her neck standing up and a slight chill.

She was being watched.

Lindsey looked sideways into the mirror, out into the room, nothing in the room mirror, but then she caught the image reflecting off of the balcony glass, to a chair near the bed.

The butterfly tattoo girl was sitting back in the chair, feet on the bed with a smile, looking directly back at her. She waved, still grinning. Pointed at herself, pointed to the chair.

As soon as Lindsey could register the chill, she'd blown a kiss and disappeared. She didn't feel threatening as much as startling.

Lindsey regained her composure and lowered herself into the last pool of solace she could expect for a while. It struck her how bizarre this whole thing was. She had lived with a girl she'd loved closer than a sister, and that girl had actually beat her to the man that she had adored from the moment she'd first saw him. Now her crazy ass was going to seal the deal between them. In any other sane scenario, this would be the time to attack.

Veronica was not alive. Not on Earth, anyway, and he was broken to the point where only Veronica had been a fix. She had no choice but to connect them.

But where's Lindsey? Who's left for her?

Not Sarah, she doesn't give a fuck. She just took an opportunity and ran with it.

Lindsey wanted to cry, but her tears had gone on vacation.

led by angels

The dimly lit burgundy room Lindsey found herself in was dark and macabre, a twist of a horror movie and a thriller. She didn't want to be in either. The floor was confusing, and gave her a sense of danger and a deep sadness. It was designed like a chess board that had been broken into levels, each row about two feet higher than the other so they almost served as stairs. A square lit in an odd hue as if a request rather than an ornament. She felt compelled to stand on the square. Several others lit, almost like pathways.

There was a tension and a streak of fear in the room, and she wasn't sure why. She also knew that she wanted to be anywhere but there. Something in her gut told her to remain alert, to remain calm. It was a fight or flight complex beginning to take hold of her, and she knew a decision had to be made.

Roger.

That fucking evil bastard.

He emerged across from her in an outfit that seemed trapped somewhere between a 1400s Renaissance leotard and a battle outfit from a space movie. But the mania of his icy psychosis was still there, that hungry drooling grin that felt like the distillation of pure evil. She watched him lick his lips, or what was left of them, and realized he was on a hunt. But this game still wasn't making sense.

Walking as if he were stalking her, he remained silent as a few rows of squares lit red, the eyes piercing through her and chilling her to the bone in an electric vibration that hurt. A moment or two passed before she realized what he held in his right hand.

A trident, with needle-sharp prongs, like something one would use at a luxury seafood restaurant to spear a meal like a savage, but battle-sized. In his grip, he spun it forcefully, not removing his eyes from Lindsey.

I'm being hunted. For real.

"Smells like fish in here, doesn't it, little girl?" He cackled at her, continually moving so it was hard for her to keep a tab on him. He was swaying almost like a drug addict in the middle of an intense high.

"You smell like fish," Roger prodded again, "Bet I know why."

"You disgusting fuckhead," Lindsey growled at him, trying to draw all of her courage up into her chest.

He laughed again, a look in his eyes something between mania and unbridled hatred. It was the insults like she'd heard before, trying to knock her down, shift her focus by forcing a panic. He knew what the vulgar talk did to her because he had done it until Jeanette had blocked him.

She had no idea what had changed, why it was no longer working.

"I'm gonna enjoy spearing that fish," he said, licking his lips slowly, "*Over and over again.*" He was massaging his crotch with his other hand for effect.

It would be difficult to get that trident away from him. She was going to have to wait until he made a move and Roger seemed to be anticipating her reaction. The survival instinct was beginning to flow into her, but her faith was the problem, just as it always had been. He had won every time, always beat her down and terrorized her.

Lindsey knew this was a dream, but she'd read somewhere if you die in your dreams, you die in real life. Or maybe that was just a horror movie premise. Either way, she hated horror movies, and this wasn't any better. Really didn't want to find out if the idea was true or not.

There seemed to be a *snap* that disrupted her attention from Roger.

The girl appeared from the right like a rush of wind, beautiful, furious. Lavender ribbons flowing from the back of a dress that seemed to drape around her like tissue paper around a telephone pole in a tornado.

She lit in front of Roger and the lights on the floor went out. "Give *that* to me," she said with hostility, ripping the trident from his hand. "Enough of this, you perverted little boy. You will leave."

Anger took over Roger's face, as if he'd been challenged to a fight. "I have a right to that," he said defiantly, pointing at Lindsey.

"You have no right to her. She's mine. You also have no right to be here, and you need to leave."

"I'm not going anywhere. I'm gonna have what's mine." Roger looked down his nose at the girl and then glanced at Lindsey again, that horrible grin retaking his face.

"I'm not asking. I'm telling. Be careful who you challenge, little boy." She spoke with a furious calm that at some points twisted in flow and power like an autotune from Hell.

They say that before a massive tsunami, there is a moment where all of the water drains from the shore as if it were being chased by a pack of wild animals. It hangs, the silence so thick you would need an axe to cut through it. All sound seems to hide under the rocks and the trees, the wind becomes as still as a pond in winter. And then the unthinkable destruction comes, howling and decimating everything in its path, as loud as the trains her father used to take her to watch at work. Lindsey felt that silence, the hairs on the back of her neck stood on end as Roger held gaze with the girl, the girl with 200 pound balls of titanium.

"Challenge? What are *you* gonna do? You want me to take ya behind the woodshed and give ya some of this, too?" He grabbed between his legs as he laughed in her face and spit. Roger moved his hand up to slap her a good one. It froze, and he looked like someone had turned on a flashlight on his face, the glow radiating his features. As the girl turned her head towards Lindsey, she saw where the light was coming from.

The girl's eyes looked like the white burning of the sun.

"*She is mine,*" the girl repeated.

Lindsey felt the wind release, picking up speed as sound hurtled into the space. The feeling of peace began filling her chest, because of what she was now seeing in front of her.

It was a look on Roger's face that Lindsey had never seen before.

Terror.

As the velocity increased, she saw the girl raise her hands over Roger like she was going to clap his ears, saw the panic and fear on his face, the trembling of his lips as he tried to speak. His face returned to normal, the bluish balloon fading away to a normal jaw, but the fear continued because he seemed to know something Lindsey didn't.

She'd never realized that you could smell in a dream. But the scent of lavender overtook the space.

Lindsey noticed one more thing she hadn't seen before, for some reason.

This girl had *wings*.

Then he was no more, visibly scattered like a bag of ashes kicked hard into the wind and gone.

The girl still held the trident. It was the subhuman booming shriek erupting from her mouth that brought Lindsey's mind back to the moment, deep and horrible, like the slamming of locomotive brakes that could never find an end. The winged girl slammed the trident into the floor and it gave way underneath them with a lurch that made Lindsey's stomach seem to lodge in her throat.

They were falling, down, down, the pieces of the strange full-sized chessboard that she had previously been standing on breaking into shattered splinters and falling faster than the speed at which they were spiraling. The rush of wind in her ears, the absolute lack of knowledge of what was below.

She didn't know if they would ever stop.

The feeling of weightlessness was almost pleasurable, like she was flying, and the girl was edging closer to her and finally pointed herself like a dart. Lindsey felt her grab both hands as they flowed down together into something that was feeling more and more ominous by the second. She watched the girl's wavy brown hair flow as if they were skydiving without helmets.

And she was beautiful.

Lindsey looked into the girl's eyes, now soft brown, so familiar. She knew she'd seen her at the airline terminal in Dallas, but this was a different familiarity, something closer to home.

"Do what must be done. You and I still have business to attend to. Call for *Corisande*."

The words hit her like a sonic charge, impacting off of her. Trying to understand what had been said to her, Lindsey realized they felt stuck into her like shrapnel.

Then everything stopped.

The next jolt she felt hit her hard, and realization struck she was in the seating across from luggage claim. One hell of a dream for that short of a nap.

Lindsey reached for her carry-on bag on the seat next to her and saw a violet butterfly had made its way inside the building and was perched on the handle.

"I don't think either of us are from around here," she gently spoke to it.

The novel butterfly slowly fanned its wings, up and down in the stream of sunlight that had fallen across her bag from the window. She decided to sit for a few moments longer. The bags could wait. She had time, and they would just spin round and round on the airport merry-go-round anyway.

way it should have been

Lindsey had been like a second daughter when she was rooming with Veronica. Maria remembered her as a very sweet but quiet girl for the most part. She'd flown out for the funeral and had spent a majority of the days she'd been in town trying to take care of Maria and the others still in the home.

She set to work like a madwoman and couldn't be stopped, arranged the food coming in from well-wishers and friends of the family, served it, cleaned the house about four days in a row. That girl she'd moved in with stayed in Los Angeles. Called twice. Whatever she said, it had made Lindsey cry. She was already crying over Veronica. Seemed rather rude.

So when she called and said she needed to meet face-to-face to talk about Veronica, it struck her as odd, but it wasn't a deniable request. Not for her, anyway.

She had met her with a hug and it just felt warm again. Maria remembered that she'd gotten Lindsey hooked on the chocolate. That might have been Veronica's doing. Her chocolate was a little different. It started with the tablet and the milk, and

Maria always added a bit of hot pepper into the mix which seemed to get rave reviews from the girls.

After they had sipped their chocolate and chit-catted, trying to catch up on things, she finally asked Lindsey what it was she had wanted to see her about. Lindsey had pulled out her phone.

"I'm not clear on how the Church would view something like what I'm about to show you. And rather than give it a big introduction, I'm going to just let you watch the video first and you can do whatever you feel you need to do with it. The only thing I'm asking for, with your approval of course, are the amethyst earrings Veronica used to wear all the time. But don't give me an answer until you see this."

She pulled out her phone and with a few taps pulled up a video. "I need you to take a breath and open your mind, because this is going to be something you are gonna think is impossible at first. This is Veronica, and it was filmed last May."

"Last May? How is that even possible?" Lindsey tapped the play button and handed over the phone.

There, on the screen was her little girl, the one whose body she'd personally identified on arrival, speaking to the camera in living color.

She watched as she heard Veronica and Lindsey speaking.

"Do you know what today's date is, and can you say it out loud?" Lindsey had asked her.

"May 5th, 2019. It's a Sunday." Veronica pointed up, "It's on the main menu widget right there."

Her little girl continued speaking.

"Jakub? When I said to get rid of your momma and take mine, I meant it. *Do it*. Worked for Jesus."

"Speaking of," Lindsey interrupted her, "Do you have anything you want to say to your mom? Not that she'll ever see this, but you never know."

"Well, Mama, if you see this, I love you, and I really miss you. I also love Jakub very much, too. If I'd had the chance, I'd have married him. So if you get to meet him, I hope you'll give him all the love you gave me and Pablo, because his momma really sucks. He needs a new one. Someone like you. I told him to take care of you, so doncha go fighting him about it. It's what I told him to do. I know how defiant you can get." She laughed.

"And just so you know, I've seen Papa and Pablo... they both look like they're doing fine. And there's some girl keeps showing up. I don't know her. She looks like those pictures of you when you and Papa first met. So everyone's okay, and now you have proof it's not a bunch of fairy tales. I love you!" Maria watched Veronica stop, and then she continued, "Where's Luna? I hope nothing bad happened to her. I trust you, whatever happened."

Maria heard the message her daughter had recorded specifically for her, but couldn't speak for a few moments. Lindsey seemed to be afraid that she'd done something horribly wrong, it was written on her face. Maria managed to choke out, "It's okay, I just need to process this. I'm very blessed that you brought this to me. It answers quite a few questions I've had lately. "

Lindsey proceeded to tell her about the plan she had come up with, a sort of memorial that would help bring closure yet again to everything that had happened. It sounded like a good plan, and she was grateful she was going to be able to help with it. Maria knew exactly who to bring in to help.

"One moment. I need to give you something," she told Lindsey.

Maria reached into the organization cubby where she kept the bills and pulled out a stack of envelopes. "I've been getting these every month, since last September. $500 each, always around the 15th, always from Austin. No return address, and they try to be secretive about who they are. I finally had one of them traced because I was getting nervous about them. Traced back to this Jakub Riser fellow. I was trying to decide what to do about it when you called. Now it's all making sense."

She laid out the envelopes in front of Lindsey and said, "I think there's about $3000 here. So let's do this. I'm going to deposit all of these and write you out a check for this amount. I want you to use this towards anything else you need to do. I'm going to also go ahead and get those earrings for you, I think she'd have wanted you to have them, anyway, so they're for you to do whatever you'd like with them."

Maria knew there was something else under the surface. She could feel it, no matter how much the girl tried to hide it.

"And the problem, if I'm sensing it correctly," Maria said, "Is that you're in love with Jakub too. Probably longer. Am I correct?"

She saw the sadness wash over her face as she tried to decide if she should be depressed or embarrassed. "He didn't want me. But he did want her. And she loves him. Who am I to get in the middle of that?"

"My beautiful girl," Maria said softly, "You don't know that." She took her dainty hands into hers and kissed them. "Let me tell you something my Mama always told me. In winter, everything sleeps. But the flowers always wake in the spring. I believe it will be the same for you. It *should* be the same for you. Problem is that you're waiting for winter, and I think you'll find it's almost spring. Don't sleep through it."

Lindsey's face scrunched as she fought off her tears and nodded. It took a few moments for her to regain her composure. And then she did what any good girl would do in this position.

She changed the subject.

"Jakub and I both know about your husband, we know about Pablo, and Jakub is making a ritual out of visiting the cemetery every August 31st."

"*That's* where the roses came from last year?"

"It would sound right for him. But we have no idea who this other girl is that Veronica's talking about here. We thought maybe it was an aunt, or maybe your mother or something."

It couldn't be. But who else would it be? There was only one other.

"No. I'm sure I know who that other girl is. *Wow.*"

halo above her head

When Veronica pushed open the plate glass doors into the sunshine, she saw a couple of soldiers seated on the parapet next to the stairs. It was a male and a female, dress blue uniforms, chatting quietly. It was the maroon berets that caught her attention. The male looked up, and spotting Veronica, nudged the female next to him and pointed.

The female promptly turned and headed towards her. As she approached within ten feet, she removed her aviator sunglasses and asked, "Veronica Salazar?"

"Yes," Veronica answered nervously.

"Lieutenant Shelaine Hester. I'm one of the advocates for Jakub Riser. Could you come with us for a moment so we can get you up to speed on everything? Nothing sinister, I promise. Your advocate sent us to collect you after Review. She thought it would be unfair to leave you unattended after you got out."

"You guys are in uniform. I didn't think that applied here," Veronica commented, confused.

Shelaine smiled, "Old habits die hard. There's nothing on Earth as cocky as a Paratrooper. We come by it honestly. Besides, nothing catches the attention like a well-decorated military uniform, right? Let's grab my husband and we'll find somewhere to talk." Leading Veronica over to the man, she saw the black rose tattoo along the right side of Shelaine's neck.

"Is there a reason for the rose tattoo there?"

"I'm an orphan. *Was* an orphan. Lost both parents when I was 16. Spent the next two years homeless because I was ducking the system. Basically fought for my life until I was 18, got my high school diploma, joined the Army on a officer path plan. They put me through college, I went Airborne. That's where I met Hester."

"I thought your name was Hester."

"It is. They just still call him Hester."

"What do they call you?"

"Ma'am, if they're smart." She snickered. "No, around here people just call me Shelaine. You can call me that. He's still Hester. He's Jakub's other advocate. We're a team. Always were, still are."

Once they reached Hester, he put out a hand and a smile and greeted her, "Sergeant First Class Hester, ma'am. Honor to meet you." He seemed to be both hard and soft simultaneously. Looked rough on the edges, but everything about him screamed that he was a professional. He gave her a solid handshake and said, "Let's move over there at that table and get comfortable for a minute." Hester gestured to a concrete picnic table under a small grove of trees.

As they slipped into the table, Hester placed himself across from Veronica and Shelaine took a seat next to her.

"So we're the advocates for Jakub, and you should probably know a little more about that and how it came to be. No better place to hear it from than the horse's mouth, yeah?" He looked to her for a reaction and continued, "So there was a different advocate in place for Jakub in the beginning, and he failed on a couple of different counts. Heavy decisions that are engineered to create a condition or create a new entry point for others is called in our parlance a *convergence point*. So a few years ago, Jakub was pointed to meet a specific person, then they would eventually have a child. This was a specific child, a directed child. But that connection didn't happen. Strike one."

He paused, surveying her for a moment, as Shelaine picked up, "The second convergence point was you. Yes, you guessed it. At the housewarming party. You were supposed to meet, connect, and later have a child. There were... *complications* with that arrangement from our side, not yours. A conflict of interests might be the best way I could describe it, so your advocate had to temporarily be re-assigned to another person. Both your new advocate as well as Jakub's advocate failed. Strike two."

Hester continued, "This is kinda a big deal. When you two connected following your exit, and I should probably point out that missing that convergence point had something to do with your exit, it created a bit of a wrinkle in things."

"What do you mean by *wrinkle*?" Veronica asked them.

"By you being deceased, and Jakub interacting with you the way he did, that unlocked some of the latent abilities we're all born with but usually have repressed. That complicates things on some levels."

"So is that a good thing, or a bad thing?"

"Both. It's good because now he will develop involuntarily to be able to communicate with those of us on this side of the veil, between carnate and incorporeal."

"He's becoming a medium," Shelaine offered, for clarification.

"Yep," Hester continued, "And that can be a good thing, but as you know, there are three arenas happening here. The incarnate world that you and Jakub and the rest of us were in when we were physically alive, the corporeal realm where we are operating now, all those woo-woo people call it the 'spirit realm', and..."

"Good grief, hon. Would you stop it with the 'woo-woo' shit? People believe what they believe, and call it what they call it. It's not like any of them can verify this until they actually get here." Shelaine shook her head at him.

"Noted, Ma'am," Hester said as Shelaine rolled her eyes. "Anyway, the space between 'em, like when you were in those goggle things we heard about, when folks have passed, but haven't crossed here, that's a really fucking sketchy area. Bad shit can happen there. Since Jakub can now tap into that, and it's already started happening, we were assigned to him. I think you already sense we're no bullshit about this venture."

"Since we've taken over this position," Shelaine said, "We've made sure to pay a good and solid amount of attention to things where *you* are concerned. It's obvious we get the relationship between you two. We understand that first hand. When he exits, you will be both requested and allowed to pick him up yourself. We call that a Retrieval Agent, and I'm sure you've talked to your kin by now and know that's what your father and brother pretty much do full-time. We think they do a damned good job of it."

"In case you didn't know, they go pick up the people nobody else wants. It's rare, but it does happen. Family excluded in your case, of course. Those guys got really good hearts, I'll tell ya that much." Hester looked at the table almost in a stare. "Jakub's headed towards a world of shit because of his abilities. That's why we were assigned. Honestly, I'm humbled that The Lady chose us to do this, so we're throwing everything we have into it, I promise you that much. We ain't leavin' shit to spare in protecting our man."

Shelaine put her hand gently on Veronica's arm and softly said, "But we do need to talk about something. There's a part of Jakub's paperwork that we're concerned you might have a bit of objection to. We can't go into all of that with you, it's not our place. When they feel it's time, The Lady will discuss that with you. It corrects the first missed convergence point because, well, *you* were the second, and you're here. But this entry *has* to happen. It's not negotiable. My gut tells me you might actually be happy when you find out. In any case, our priority in all things is Jakub first, before all things, including you. Even if we try to factor you in the decision 99%. Bottom line is that when he exits, it's you two. All you two."

"And we'll be together, like you guys?"

Hester scrunched his face, "*Kinda* like us. You know how Shelaine outranks me? She's an officer, I'm an NCO, which by the way, was highly illegal the way we did it, but in a way that'll make more sense later, Jakub will outrank *all* of us. He and The Lady are connected. He just doesn't know that yet. Hell, you and The Lady are connected. We can't go into that, either."

"It'll be almost like being married into royalty, if that helps," Shelaine said.

"Except this one's *real*," Hester finished.

"So what do I do now?"

"Enjoy everything, I guess. I'm not really sure. You'll have to talk to your advocate. You do have a very good one, although she's not really your advocate anymore. I mean, you'll probably talk to her for a while, get some training, go off to do some fun job for a bit until Jakub exits. That would be my guess."

"So you're saying I'm kinda left to my own devices?"

"Well, yeah. Maybe you could hang with us for a while. We don't mind, But if anything stupid happens, you'll need to hide out of sight while we work."

"I think I can handle that. So who exactly is this Lady you keep talking about?"

"I am," said a soft, musical voice, as a girl slid in next to Hester.

Veronica recognized her immediately. She was the girl that kept coming to the glass when Veronica was trapped in the VR headset.

Veronica still had no clue who she was or how they were connected. It was written all over her face, and The Lady wasn't really certain what to tell her. Some things could certainly wait, and in fact this would *need* to wait.

There is a question that we all must sometimes ask ourselves.

How far will you push a friend, if you know that what is at the end of their suffering is better than all of the pain combined in their journey to get through it?

Sometimes it can be a question of mercy, other times, it's a factor of their longevity and endurance. She wasn't quite sure what the Hesters had told Veronica, but knowing them, it was strictly professional and no cats were out of the bag just yet. That was why she had picked them.

Dependability. Integrity.

All of the plans looked good, but the fact of the matter remained that emotions *were* involved, the hardest and the strongest ones, the feelings that were electrical impulses that once created would last through space and time for eons.

There was a theory once that if you could shoot an arrow from a bow, and there were no forces or impediments to alter its ability to travel, it would fly forever.

Love can be like that.

At least it's nice to pretend. And little Veronica kept wandering along with her, chattering away about her life story not quite fully realizing that she had been there next to her for most of it.

Except for that thing with Corisande. She had to deal with that girl after she got wrapped up under a steering wheel and none of the authorities could explain why. Nor would the young man she'd been traveling with properly explain how his pants got down to his knees before he was forcefully ejected from the vehicle.

Then the tiny fact of explaining all of this to her fiancé, who was not in the car at the time, and unclear as to Cori's whereabouts.

That's a pristine example of damage control. But then again, Corisande still to this day probably didn't realize she was in the car with a state senator's son.

Hence, the damage control.

"When will I get to see Jakub again?" Veronica asked. The question burned. There was so much the girl didn't know, didn't understand yet.

A lot of it was because she was so fresh, and the emotions coupled with the almost selfish individuality dampened what love was, and all it could be. She had to be patient with her former charge. Veronica didn't even quite grasp that she wasn't the same person that she was on Earth just yet. It was partially because her awakening had happened in the Middle Zone, but at least she was safely within what was essentially an electrical appliance when that happened.

It was difficult in her position, having to think of everyone under you, the charges under them, trying to always work for everyone's' best good. Things get tangled up, crossed around. Incarnate life doesn't afford the ability to see the different sides and experiences as it does afterwards.

"You will see him again very soon." She paused. Maybe it was time to start warming her up to the idea of what was coming. It was only fair. "You've heard that saying that if you love something, set it free, if it comes back, it's meant to be?"

"I already don't like where this is headed."

"I would imagine not, but there is a reality to things. I understand how you feel about him. I understand why. In fact, I support and applaud it. At one time, you were meant to be with him." She looked deep into Veronica's eyes to force the emphasis, "And that's why you will be his Retrieval Agent. You're going to have plenty of time together, don't worry about that. You know, love matures and intensifies on this side. I can give you a good example of what I mean. Take the Hesters, for instance. Shelaine and Hess *do* love each other, just like they did when they were alive. And they make an *incredible* amount of sex jokes. But they're both hardened soldiers. That was part of their culture and communication. The love they have now is much, much deeper and more intense than something you'd get in a bedroom. That's why they work. That's why I think you two will work. But that won't happen for a while. Jakub still has to live the rest of his life. He has important things to accomplish, and one of them includes something you would have an issue with today. But it has to and *will* happen. You're going to have to understand and get used to that idea. I'm going to make sure you get your day, but you're eventually going to have to step back for a little while."

She saw the crest-fallen look in her eyes. This was always the hardest part, but she'd never had to have a discussion quite like this.

"I know, Baby Girl. But that's not all you need to get this in perspective."

"Oh, shit. There's more?"

"Yes, there's more. You and Jakub are not the same. He's my kind."

"I don't understand. What do you mean *your kind*?"

"There is a slight difference in the spiritual spark. There is a common misconception that protectors are just a higher rank than those who are advocates or do retrieval, or any of the other jobs we do to keep things going from this realm. That's not entirely accurate. We are actually formed differently. Think of it as the difference between your favorite puppy and a wolf. In the right circumstances, they play in the pen just fine together. But sometimes the difference becomes obvious."

"He's a wolf."

"He *is* a wolf. And so am I. So we are directly connected. We are *Wilwarin Nosse*, the butterfly clan. So the way things work is that you have various little clans, little cliques that form. One could usually go in and out of them, I imagine, but when it comes to the Wilwarin, we have several different sects, but they aren't opposed to each other. They're basically the same thing. I think you say 'brother from another mother', or 'sister from a different mister'? Same concept. You don't have battles in the corporeal realm. We have no reason or desire to fight each other. Time goes on over there, and we just do what we do. One day you're eating grass, then the next you're splitting atoms. It's kinda all the same to us, except we keep rotating on the incarnate side to try and be helpful. That's really it."

"And that's why I keep seeing butterflies."

"It is."

"Then what about the lavender? I smell it everywhere I go."

"That's because you are with me. I *adore* lavender. It's part of my essence. I like the roses too, don't get me wrong. But I love lavender. And purple."

"I *love* purple."

"And yet another reason why you're so awesome, Baby Girl. Purple is the color of royalty, among other things. I want to show you a queen. A queen that I love most deeply. I love you, too, don't ever misunderstand that. But I am linked to her very closely, and I love her, and cry for her, and hope for her. So when I was pulled away from you as an advocate, I helped form and train the perfect advocate for her. And she is an exemplary creature, let me tell you. I'm *very* proud of my Corisande."

"So Corisande is not the queen?"

"No. But you know her. And you need to see her for who she is, and realize what she came from. I think it's important. And so we're going to take a step back in time. I'm going to make you watch *all* of this."

"What am I watching," Veronica asked guardedly.

"You'll see. Because you have to in order to understand why you will need to step away for a bit."

The environment faded around them to a street with a row of houses on it. The houses sat adjacent to a railroad track, and the town itself looked to be a small town, no large buildings, only enough concrete and road tar as was utterly necessary.

As The Lady guided her to a specific house, she saw the tan paint and forest green shutters. A man stood leaning against the edge of the house, laughing lowly and facing the backyard. A thin pale girl with long light blonde hair stood in the middle of a ring of five other girls. She looked confused, out of place.

They paced the girl like a pack of ravenous coyotes, moving in a circle as she tried to understand what was happening. The air was thick, and the tension could be felt riding on it like a wave of danger. She turned just enough so that Veronica could finally get a good look at the girl's face. She was young, maybe fifteen or sixteen.

"That's Lindsey!" Veronica said breathlessly.

search the stars

Nothing brings joy into young boy's hearts like the sight of cold glass bottles. They always mean something good, something important, almost like a liquid crack cocaine with bubbles in it.

Sugar.

Getting the permission to actually drink them is another victory, like Douglas MacArthur in the Philippines. Momma and Daddy might reassign them to play in the front yard, but by Jove they were gonna storm the damned beach and return.

Aiden headed straight to the kitchen without stopping as if he were on a divine mission while Willie helped Jakub get the cases of soda placed out of the reach of small hands. Jakub heard him boom, "And on the Seventh Day, the Lord said, 'Let there be breakfast tacos'..."

Willie grinned and said snidely to Jakub, "Done tole ya, we goan' make off with 'im. All ya gotta do is feed 'im right."

He reappeared with his hands full. "They preparin' for an army. You better get it before it's gone. They got chorizo, egg and potato, and looks like carnitas. And you don't hafta ask *me* twice. I'm puttin' a dent in this program."

As he was talking, Willie headed out the back door towards the deck.

"Hey, I need you back here, Aiden," Willie yelled, "Gotta talk to ya for a few minutes." They both began moving towards the back door when Willie cranked at Jakub, "Not you, numbnuts. Just your buddy here."

"Well, I do feel the love," Jakub said sarcastically.

"She's in one of her moods lately," Carl said, "Ya might wanna come with me. We'll find something kinda useful to burn off time. It'll keep us from getting eaten."

Whatever it was Willie had said to Aiden on the back steps, it had certainly left him nonplussed. He could see the gears grinding in his head and Aiden only seemed to have one word to offer him, "*Wow.*"

"That's really all you gotta say? 'Wow'? Tell me she didn't just hit on you."

"Oh, god no," He said mortified, "She ain't gonna do anything like that. But I can tell ya that you must be like the fricking Golden Child or something."

"Oh, shit, what are they gonna do to me?"

"I don't think it's as much do *to* you as do *for* you."

"Okay, what are they gonna do *for* me?"

"Nuh-uh, you ain't implicatin' me in that. I ain't tellin' ya nuthin'. They've already recruited me. I know when to pick my battles, and I got the good sense to not fight back and sass your sister."

He knew better than that, too. It was better to just let that sleeping dog lie. When Willie committed to plans, you just stayed out of it. She was like the Tasmanian Devil, and getting in the middle could be a risk for injury.

Still didn't staunch his curiosity.

Willie knew what was in her brother's mind. She always did. "I know you have a problem with patience," she began, "But just this one time, you'll wanna go with it. I don't think you're going to be prepared for it, but it has to be one of the best things that can possibly be given to you. Just trust me."

"You know I always trust you. Who else am I gonna trust?"

"Well, there's Carl. And Aiden, and Li-luh-ther people."

"Excuse me? Didn't catch that." Willie sounded like she had a ping-pong ball in her mouth.

"Other people. People you don't know you can trust, but soon will. Okay?"

"Okay."

"Now it's time to go punish some kids with sugar."

"I thought you said that was punishing *you*."

"I don't play football. Carl plays football, so the joke's on you. And I know he is, because they're gonna be playing about twenty minutes after they drink those sodas you brought."

"How do ya know?"

"Because I just said so. Keep up with the conversation. By the way, didja see anything on your credit report that Mom tried to do to ya?"

"Nope. Everything is normal. I guess it's only you. She knew I'd wipe it out real quick. She stood a much better chance with you, and probably thought that with the kids, you wouldn't be paying attention. I bet she still hasn't caught on that you know."

"Yeah, I think I'll just let that one ride for now. So don't go planning any big trips for the next month. I got plans for you."

"What kinds of plans?" Jakub asked.

"Doesn't matter. Plans are plans, and when I make 'em they should be adhered to. After all, didn't I ask you to trust me?"

"And I said I trusted you."

"Then make sure you stick around. And make sure that Lincoln salesman don't go nowhere, either. I already talked to 'im. You make sure he pays attention."

"Aiden? I can't tell him shit."

"Sure you can. I did. It better damned well work, too." Aiden had strolled back into the room with the kids following. "I mean it," Willie said, pointing a finger at him, "You better do what I tole ya. Or there'll be no more carnitas. You'll be sitting on the front porch all sad."

"Jakub has brisket."

"You'll need teeth to eat it, buddy," she countered with a grin. "And you, young mister," She said, turning to face Jakub, "You need to get yourself a suit. Like the kinds with a tie and stuff."

"Why?"

"Because every man needs to own a suit. That's why."

"She's about to preach!" Carl called out from the living room sofa, where he'd laid back to escape the whirlwind he was married to.

"Hallelujah," Jakub muttered sarcastically.

"Boy, you shut up," Willie said with a smirk.

"I don't own a suit," Aiden offered.

Willie puffed up her chest with false bravado and replied, "Another outburst like that from *you*, young man, and I'll take ya out behind the shed and beat ya again!"

"Didn't hurt that bad the first time. But my hair, don't touch my hair," he played, touching his head.

"I'll shave your ass. Have people wondering which one of the Three Stooges you are."

"So you're sayin' I need to get a suit, but you ain't even going to have decency to tell me why?"

"I *did* tell you why. Because I said so. Because I'm the momma hen around these parts, and when I say so, *I say so*."

"But I ain't from these parts. I live in Austin."

"Son, I don't give a damn if you live on the moon. You're in my kitchen. Buy a damned suit."

"Yes, Mom."

"Hey. *Hey*! Don't you go givin' me no sass around here! Who you think you're talkin' to?"

Jakub shook his head, "And who you beatin' up?" His grin made her crack. She never could hold this act up for too long, but it was the way Willie was. She pretended to be the tough momma, knocking everyone around. Her bark was generally worse than her bite. Mess with her family, and you'd really find out what her bite was like. And it came with a lot less talking.

"Seriously. Buy a suit. One ya like. Black'll fit every occasion. But ya gotta make sure it's one you *really* like, because you're gonna need it soon. Like in the next month. I'm sorry I can't tell ya much more than that, and don't ya go jerking with Aiden tryin' to make him cough it up, neither. Let that dog lie, and you'll be a lot happier ya did."

the force of the blow

It was the first drink Darcy had consumed in months. She didn't really know why she had quit, it happened one day, and she didn't think much about it. But what happened yesterday, in the park, she just wanted to steady herself a bit and chew it.

The girl from the Statesman was speaking to Darcy. She seemed less happy than the last time she'd seen her. This time she was more direct, more business-like, almost.

"You're aware that you have an advocate that's responsible for helping you actuate many of the things that are supposed to occur when you're incarnate, correct?"

"Well, yes. Guides, you mean?"

"You can call them guides, if you like. No law against it. But sometimes they don't do what they're supposed to be doing. Sometimes they act directly *against* your best interests. Know that those practices are very highly frowned upon. There can be... *consequences* for actions like that. It's almost like a state of active war against the one you're supposed to be directing and protecting." She seemed very irritated, and growing more so by the moment.

"Usually, you won't be able to see them directly unless a dispensation has been allocated that allows it. That's somewhat rare, but not unheard of. You remember back at the bar when we first met, and I asked if you saw a man by the window?"

"Yes," Darcy responded, trying to wrap her mind around what she was hearing.

"Well, here's the problem. You have a dispensation to see these advocates, guides as you call them, not just for you, but for everyone else. It's part of your path and your plan. Because you're supposed to teach these talents to Mr. Riser. Ya can't teach what ya can't do. I wondered why, since it's clear that you have an allocation. Now I know why. Your advocate has actively blocked you being able to see him. He's turned that gift off that I personally directed you to have. I have a problem with that."

"But I can see you," Darcy said, confused.

"Ah, dearie, but I'm not an advocate. I'm a protector."

Darcy pulled back, not understanding. The girl smiled sweetly and looked deep into her eyes. It was so intense she felt as if she were falling deep into a well just by looking at her.

"The difference is that, in your lingo, I'm not a guide. I'm an angel. You know how all of your relationships seem to fall flat and none of it ever goes right, even though you want them to?"

"Yes. I'm very unlucky in the love department."

"Sabotaged, you mean."

"What?"

"You're being sabotaged, torpedoed. Your advocate, instead of advocating for you and your better good, has become your antagonist and thinks you will never find out about it until it's all too late and you've exited here. I think that's a pretty horrid way to treat someone, don't you?"

The words were beginning to sink in. She wasn't unlucky as much as she was being psychically abused. It was all starting to make sense, almost like a hex had been put on her.

"I'd like to give you that gift back that you're supposed to have. Correct some wrongs. So you can have the other gift I'm trying to give you. Jealousy is a very ugly thing, and an evil monster that needs to be choked and stamped out everywhere we find it, wouldn't you agree?"

"Yes, I would."

As the girl moved in closer, the lavender scent grew stronger.

"What I am about to do is going to be uncomfortable. Usually this would happen in your sleep, but your advocate over there has no idea what I'm saying to you right now, and I'll keep it that way until you can talk to him yourself. I need to do this now, and open your eyes another level. You're going to feel this in the center of your head. Just breathe, stay still, and it'll pass."

The girl reached her left hand around to the base of Darcy's skull, and the right hand over her eyes. As the girl closed her eyes and breathed in, Darcy felt as if she were standing in the eye of a tornado, the rush and the swirling seeming to encircle them.

And then the pain began, like a single flame in the center of her skull, burning, electric. She couldn't place the taste that had formed in her mouth, almost like a combination of burning plastic and metal. The heat felt like it was forming behind her eyeballs, growing, the pressure making her wince.

"Easy, we're almost done," the girl said.

The pressure grew, and with a tiny *pop*, Darcy felt like she had been dunked in a pool of water. Wet, cool, dripping. Feeling the subtle changes in the air as it blew around her.

"That should do it," the girl said, "Now you're back on track, and you can see what you've been missing."

"Thank you," Darcy said breathlessly, not certain what it was she would soon see.

"Not a problem," the girl cooed, "But sadly, it's yet another moment in which I have to show Pretty Boy over there why I outrank his punk ass."

She removed her hand.

In front of Darcy, about twenty feet away was a casually observing, smirking Clayton Stanton. He had a look of a cat that had just swallowed a baby bird.

She blurted automatically, "Why the fuck is *he* here?"

Darcy felt the weight in the pit of her stomach as she realized all in one moment, those days of happiness, those moments of joy, all of the recovery and the pain she'd worked so hard to resolve, be rid of, and to begin anew were each shredded into nothingness by a single person. A man she'd trusted in life, mourned in death, and had tried on many teary, painful nights to make peace with. He was supposed to be her friend and lover, but the best he'd given her was the attention of a mortal enemy.

The next emotion she felt came in hot as a cutting torch.

Unbridled rage.

"You did all this to me?" She hissed, barley able to contain herself.

Clayton's mouth flapped as if he was trying to say something and couldn't get the words together. It was a look, a reaction of surprise. He looked like a man that had been caught in bed with his mistress by the media.

"Y-you can see me?"

"Clear as day," Darcy said, "And you've got a lot of explaining to do. But honestly, right now, I don't want to hear it. I don't want to hear your voice. *At all.* Just shut up until I calm down."

As she tried to regain her composure, she realized the girl was gone.

seeing is not believing

The heat blew through him like standing in front of a blast furnace or a pizza oven, Jakub couldn't tell which. But this time, he *felt* them before he saw them.

"Know where ya at, son?" He heard Hester's voice say from behind his right shoulder.

Iraq. Has to be.

"Give the kid twenty points, he's earned it," Hester said. "I know you've been wondering ever since you met us, because it's one thing to tell you a story, but it's something completely different to actually show you the story."

"We don't like comin' here," Shelaine said, "Only been here twice since that day..."

"That'd be the place we got turned into confetti right over there," Hester said, pointing at a portion of the dirt hardback road that looked almost washed out.

"I do appreciate it, but *why* bring me here? I imagine you're going to tell me the story, for which I'm gonna be grateful, but you guys don't do anything without a reason, so..."

"I'm not gonna stand here and blow smoke up yer ass, kid," Hester said, "The places we're going on your trip will be *fucked*. That's why we're here to begin with. It's basically the world we know, just different aggressors. Good news is that you'll end up about like an Oreo cookie. Two good sides on the top and bottom, with a lotta squishy in the middle. We're concerned with the squishy. After all, you know Murphy's Law?"

"Um, no... wait. They used to say that a lot in Killeen."

Hester jerked, "You were at Fort Hood?" He looked confused, "I don't remember seein' that in your..."

"Naw," Jakub said, "I went to school out there for a while. Same little junior college thing a lot of the Army folks there use. Something about 'if something can go wrong, it will go wrong'."

"Good. Then you're a step ahead on today's lesson. But there's more than one law. Like in the case of the cookie I was talking about, 'The only good things in life are either illegal, immoral, or fattening'. There's also that other one, 'Never sleep with anyone crazier than you'."

"And yet, I did," Shelaine hammered. Hester intentionally held back a reaction. He just shrugged in acknowledgment and replied, "And how'd that work out for ya, miss?"

"Still here," she answered.

The two of them seemed to Jakub to click on their own wavelength so tightly that he'd be utterly amazed if they hadn't been able to read each other's minds when they were alive. Apparently this state brought it even closer.

"I know I didn't explain it before, because you've never seen us in uniform, but Shelaine outranks me pretty heavily. She's a First Lieutenant, and at the time of this shitshow was promotable to Captain. So she's part of the riggers, the folks that pack the 'chutes. I on the other hand was a Sergeant First Class and a Jumpmaster. So she packs 'chutes, I throw fuckers off the plane. Easy concept. She was over in Quartermasters, and I was a Devil in Baggy Pants. A grunt. Still meant it was illegal as fuck for us to get married. Army didn't know. They had it on paper, but the way they had it on paper, they didn't connect the dots. It woulda been a matter of time. Technology was startin' to get a bit too advanced for comfort."

"I was gettin' out anyway. Didn't have any plans to hang onto my commission. Then I coulda done some other work and it wouldn't have been a big deal. Once he ETS'd, we'd be free."

"ETS?" Jakub asked.

"Expiration Term of Service. When you get cut loose from the Army. For enlisted guys, anyway," Hester said. "We were doing crazy shit when we were stateside. Accidentally meeting up at the same hotels, weekend retreats, finally she got an apartment about 20 miles away from post, and we moved in together. I kept my mail and room at the barracks, so nobody really had anything to go on."

"I don't understand why it was illegal."

"An officer and an enlisted person are okay if they married before they came into service, but if they're already in when they meet as single folks, it's no-contact. Complete no-go. Called fraternization, and actually has civil and criminal penalties involved that can get really heavy."

"So how do you two end up here together?"

"We were leaving the same general place, and going to the same general destination, and since no one else, or at least very few people knew we were a thing, it wasn't a question for me to be riding with him. Besides, you're always good to two people, the guy that cooks your meals, and the guy that packs your chute. So a favor to a rigger, especially the one in charge of 'em, was perfectly normal."

"There were four of us, plus the gunner, Galveson. Like your beach, no 't'. Good kid. Corporal Rogers was the only one that made it, took off a leg and an arm. Keegan was driving. Neither of us had a chance. You see those stone pillars there?" Hester pointed off to the left, where what used to be a whitestone arch stretched over the road, "That was the entry point for us, everything to the right is headed to PogueLand."

"PogueLand?"

"The rear echelons, where I usually worked, with the other *FOBbits*, I believe your boys called us," Shelaine said with a smirking eye to Hester, "It's all the support units that provide services to the combat units. We were fine until right there. IED got us directly under the vehicle. We weren't in a troop transport. Damned near no armor on it. Pretty stupid, now that I think about it."

"But now you see what happened, and that was kinda the point. So we should probably get to the next point. What do you know about yourself? What do you feel?"

"How ya mean?"

"Well, do you ever feel like you were built for something else, that you're supposed to be doing something else other than what you're doing right now?"

"I don't really know what I think. I don't even know what I think about running into you two all the time."

"Well, it'll be a while, but you'll get to where you can see us all the time, even in waking life. One of the talents you've now been blessed with. It just has to develop. We'll be first. There'll be others. Eventually you'll also be able to see Veronica. Trust me, the world's gonna look pretty crowded at that point."

"I'll be on the lookout for amateur tattoo artists," Jakub said. Hester snickered.

"Probably a good idea."

"So exactly how did that happen? Just so I don't wake up with the Longhorns tattooed on *my* ass."

"Hey, I didn't do the actual tattooing. I was just an untrained medical assistant looking out for the well-being of a lonely troop."

"You tattooed his ass," Shelaine snorted.

"It was a cry for help."

"I don't see how. Who actually did it, anyway?"

"Smiley. Of course, with a name like that, it wasn't a big surprise he was an alcoholic. Sergeant Edwin Smiley. With a name like that, you don't need a cock-blocker or a pair of Buddy Holly birth control glasses. The name does it all."

"That was the medic, right? He was actually a decent looking guy," Shelaine said.

"Yeah, he used to say his name was Shaun Wilson when he was at the clubs. Made things easier. But yeah, he was an absolute lush. Drunkest guy I ever saw use a syringe." Hester shook his head and grinned, "Had a five gallon tub of peanut butter next to his desk. I wondered what it was for once, and that's when I got introduced to the office favor."

"Office favor?" Jakub looked quizzically.

"Okay, so if you had to go get a shot or check up or anything from Smiley, and he didn't have to work at sick call that morning... you know how doctors' offices always have the suckers out for ya. This was the Smiley Sucker. And we literally called it that. He does whatever he has to do with you, and then you get to knock down two shots of whatever liquor you choose. He usually had whiskey, vodka, and some high end clear shit you melt plastic and paint with. You knock your shots, you get a big honkin' plastic spoonful of peanut butter. You get to keep the spoon. He always had a shiny metal one of his own in there. Ya don't fuck with his spoon. And he always smelled like peanuts."

"He gave me a shot in the ass once. I swear he was so fucked that he didn't know his own area code, but I watched him give me that shot in my ass. Didn't feel a damned thing. Watched him shoot that shit in, and it was like he did nothin'. I told him, 'What the hell? I didn't feel a thing!' And that crackpot just looked at me, grinned, and said, 'That's because I'm a badass. You want the brown stuff, or the firewater today?' Yeah, I wasn't arguing with that guy. And Buckner now belongs to the Navy. Don't really feel bad about that. Kid was a prick anyway."

Hester dropped into thought and snorted again.

"You could give Smiley either a ten-dollar-bill on a Friday, or two twenties a month on payday, and he'd show up on Sunday mornings at the barracks with an IV and a bottle of Mountain Dew. He called it the Smiley Hangover Service. It's fucking amazing the secrets troops will keep for the right service. Yeah, I was a regular customer for a while. I hear he did it for the First Sergeant a time or two."

"Corps had responsibility on the gate and the road the night before." Shelaine paused, changing the subject. "You can't really blame them too much, but tactically it was an idiot move. Everything was put into motion for the perfect disaster. It was cold as hell the night before, desert weather's crazy. Days are blistering, nights are frigid. You'd be amazed the dips and dives temps take out here. So the legs had some kids out here, and they were concerned about them being out here too long. You have an obligation to keep an eye on that crap. So I get it. We'd have never done it, but I get it. They pulled 'em and moved 'em about a half mile that way, around that bend there," she said, pointing to the right.

"Insurgents came in, dug up that point right there and placed their little present," Hester finished.

"What do you remember," Jakub asked, "Like, how was the passing?"

"Well," Shelaine said, "I really didn't have much to it. Me and Hess were talkin', and then there was a jerk, and something like a light switch had been flipped."

"Veronica said that for her it was like being sucked into a fan."

"I could see that. I think the last thing I remember was lookin' into Hess's eyes, and the loud boom."

"I was turned around in my seat, back to the window. That's a rarity for me. But I could look in her eyes all day, which mighta been my downfall, not that it had anything to do with anything. One second I'm lookin' at her, next second we're outside the vehicle over there," Hester said, pointing, "and there's junk metal and body parts everywhere."

"There was two people standing there in normal everyday clothes, sayin' it was time to go. And I remembered hearing somewhere that you should always go to the light when you die, and no shit, there it was." She giggled, "And I'll never forget what Hess said next..."

"Oh, god," Jakub said, "What did he say?"

"Well, I always have something stupid for every occasion I guess, so..." he was actually hesitating.

"*Welp*," Shelaine imitated with bravado, "*I guess we're doin' the Stargate thing now...*"

"The point you need to take away from this is that there's a whole world out here that's wrapped around the one you're in, and you're gonna learn more than ya ever wanted to know about it. Also, things can change on a dime. There's no real guarantee on anything in life. Soon you'll see that there's more to the people around you than you originally thought, and I'm sure that'll make things very interesting for you."

"I've seen part of it, with the whole Garry deal. I swear that guy looked as real as anyone else. I had no idea I was talking to a ghost. Sometimes I wonder just how many of them I see now on a daily basis."

"Probably more than you think. And in many cases, it won't matter. You are only supposed to help a certain number of them, pretty much the ones that come to you, or the ones you're directed to. We help with some of that. But I promise you there are more things out there than your garden variety straggler ghost. You'll end up seeing more of those before this gets done. All part of your training. After all, you're going to have some big shoes to re-fill."

"Re-fill?"

"You're actually a different sort of soul than many of us. That won't make sense right now, and honestly it doesn't have to. We just have to make sure to escort you right back to the discovery of that fact, and the road is gonna be like this one here. Nice stretches that seem familiar until something goes 'bang'."

"And when it goes bang?"

"That's what we're here to help prevent. Soon, you're gonna be told by someone you don't expect to go to a specific place. Do it. Don't argue, don't question, you can trust that person with your life.

And you probably should. You two have a lot in common. You have common needs, and it might be smart to let go and jump in. And no, I don't mean Darcy. Or Veronica."

"I'm gonna go back to my first question," Hester said again, "Do you feel something in you that tells you you're different from most people, like something inside you is very clearly not the same?"

"It's there, I just can't put my finger on it. It feels almost like it was locked away for a reason. Kinda like those Christmas presents you knew was in the closet, but also knew you'd get your ass beaten if you pulled them out and looked at them. Know what I mean?"

"Yeah, that was kinda what I was diggin' for. You have a similarity to our boss. In fact, if all goes according to plan, you'll be *our* boss one day."

"So I guess it's a good idea for you guys to do a real good job."

"You bet your ass it is," Shelaine answered. "We'd still do the best job we could possibly do, even if that wasn't the case, since that's just the way we're wired, but in this specific case, we really have a motivation to help you release your inner badass. Which is why we're here showing you all of this crap. You'll see uglier, but now you know where we've been, it helps you put a bit of direction on your compass."

"Squishy stuff," Hester said, "Just remember the squishy stuff. It's white, sweet, and creamy. But ya wouldn't wanna try to swim an ocean of it, now wouldja?"

limosine fist fight

"You're taking all of this way too far to the point that people are just gonna think you're crazy. If you keep all of this bullshit up, no one in their right mind's gonna want to talk to you, or have anything else to do with you. I thought you'd gotten past all of this stupid crap, but I guess not."

Lindsey wasn't acting normal and some sense had to be talked into her before she screwed up everything. All of this traipsing around the country chasing rocks and babbling to people about her dead friend. It was cute for a while, but now it was just getting boring and in some cases infuriating to put up with.

It was like her lovely little arm candy had slipped a gear, and that was no good. People were gonna figure out that she was crazy, and that would not look good at all. Pretty soon they would lump Sarah in and think she was crazy, too. She'd worked way too hard to get where she was, build all the right connections, and be seen where it mattered to have this silly girl just tear it all down.

She didn't respond. She rarely ever did. It was boring, sometimes it was like kicking around a sack of flour that just never fought back. She was all looks and no brain anyway. But Lindsey had been different since she went to Texas.

Sarah realized she probably should have talked her out of it while she still had the chance, but now she was good and messed up from that trip to Texas. There was really only one way to work this to her advantage.

"Alright, fuck it. I'll play along," Sarah said, trying to heighten the sweetness in her voice. Better to catch flies with honey than vinegar.

"With what?" Lindsey asked.

"We'll go out there together, at least you'll have some moral support with all those strangers. That bunch won't be like your friends from work. They're a totally different type of people. You should have picked up on that by now. Can't really trust 'em. With all those guns in Texas, you're lucky nobody's shot you yet."

Lindsey remained silent. She looked for an expression to work off of, but there really wasn't one.

"I'll cover the costs, you won't have to worry about any of that. Then you can use the rest of it on this whole memorial thing and it can be put to bed for everybody. Maybe then he can quit carrying that dumb fucking rabbit everywhere he goes. I mean, god, he's a grown man, not a fucking 8-year-old kid."

The fire that lit in her eyes meant she'd hit a sore spot. That was good. She was even easier to convince when she was angry. She'd get rattled and quit thinking things out. Then they could get this whole thing over with and back to normal.

"Do you already have the flights picked out?"

"*A* flight. You said you weren't gonna go."

"Well, then this is what we'll do. We'll cancel yours, and I'll use the company card to schedule two flights there and back." Sarah knew that Lindsey had added another day before coming back, and she was going to make sure to screw up whatever the plan was. After all, she hadn't been consulted on any of this, and it both messed with her schedule and left her wondering what Lindsey was up to. She had to be able to know where Lindsey was at and what she was doing if this relationship was going to work right.

"Alright," Lindsey exhaled. "I'll cancel it, but you have to get your set of tickets first. I have to have a ticket in my hand that is good before I'm canceling *anything*."

Sarah smiled. *I win again*, she thought.

"So when is it?"

"Thursday after next."

"Okay. So we'll fly in Wednesday night and then back out Thursday night. We'll only need to spend one day out there."

"No. I'll have to go Tuesday night. Wednesday's gonna be packed making sure everything is together for Thursday. I'm not the only person involved in this, and if you'd done half the shit you said you'd do, you would know that."

"I don't think it's that serious. Wednesday should be fine."

"Then I'm using my own damn ticket, and I might just go extend it another day. Not like I'm in a rush, and I have the vacation time."

"Okay, okay. Tuesday night, then. But we have to come back Thursday. I hafta have my boss' deposition ready by Friday."

It was a lie, but how the hell would Lindsey know that? She had nothing to do with the legal field. A deposition here, a hearing there, having to stay late to redline documents, which was actually done by the secretaries, but the dumb bitch didn't know that. After all, she was a fucking blonde. She was lucky to get into doors by herself. And all of those added up to free time to do more exciting things.

I don't hide a black book in my desk at work for nothing.

Lindsey seemed a little hurt, but she'd get over it. She always did. Play the game right, and you always get something close to what you wanted out of it.

There were things that she had wanted out of this relationship. She'd seen how Lindsey had wanted that boy so damned bad, saw the weakness, the confusion. She wanted someone to want her like that. To be perfectly honest, Sarah just wanted *anyone* to want her. So the only way to get around it, to salve that pain and that need was to do a little bit of skin marketing and make them want her.

It had worked with Lindsey, because she had barely known what planet she was on, so meek and timid, so unbelievably easy. She was the beautiful low-hanging fruit that no one else had gone after because they didn't think they could get her.

Their ignorance was Sarah's bliss.

She loved her, and hated her at the same time. Wanted her to be free, but needed her locked down close so she wouldn't get away. These trips scared the living piss out of Sarah, because they would turn out like her relationships before.

Someone goes out of your line of sight, then the next thing you know, they're packing their shit and disappearing into the sunset arm in arm with someone else.

"How are ya holdin' up, Cori?"

She shook her head and rolled her eyes. This was all going a new level of stupid.

"I swear, I wanna slap one upside the head to knock some sense into her, and punch the other in the face because, well, she deserves it. How's Hess?"

"Babysitting. I guess that's probably a bad way to say it. We really like this kid, and given where he comes from, it's kinda like being a Presidential bodyguard. Like the Secret Service or something. Not that I ever liked those guys, but still."

"Lady sure knows how to direct traffic."

"That she does. She always makes ya feel like you just got a promotion." Shelaine was sitting on the other end of the couch from Corisande, watching the two girls have their spat in the kitchen.

"Is she always like this?" Shelaine asked, pointing at Sarah.

"You mean a cunt? Yeah, always. I know what she does after work. She needs some good back alley dentistry with a heavy rusted wrench."

"That's a bit harsh."

"She's a bit of a scoundrel hussy bitch."

"She *is* pretty."

"Pretty gets you some ass. Doesn't solve much else. That girl's a hot mess. I don't know of many good solutions for her."

"Maybe she's in the wrong place?"

"Girl, I *know* she's in the wrong place. Tell me something I don't know. That one's a little snake. Thing is, she has the potential to not be. Doesn't keep me from being any less pissed off at her."

"You been able to talk to Lindsey yet?"

"No. I can't seem to get her to make the connection. She's blocked everything off because of that dickhead, and won't open back up. Calling in the cavalry worked, but she still won't open up. She's like my special little clam. How's your boy?"

"I gotta take him shopping."

Cori laughed out loud, "Come again?"

"I have to take him clothes shopping."

"How does that work?"

"I whisk him off to the mall and force him to put on clothes until I'm happy."

"What does Hess think about that?"

"He loves it. Bastard. Then again, if it's not military issue, I have to dress him, too. It was his idea. I asked him why he didn't just go out with him, Boy's Day Out, and he said, 'Why? I make you dress *me*. Whadda I have to do with this?' So that's how it's gonna be, I guess. It'll be fun. I haven't been to a mall in a while, and it'll be fun to torture yet another male."

"He'll spend all day staring at your boobs."

"That's Hess. Jakub's seemed to have gotten over it. But yeah, it's a good tool to have in your arsenal, I guess. I'll need it for the salesmen at the mall. Provided they're straight, of course."

"I still can't believe she is *so* unable to play charades."

"Who, Lindsey?"

"Yeah! I mean, it's right there next to you, that chair there, with the leather and the wood handles. That's her chair. She doesn't allow anyone else to sit in it. Jakub sat in it once. You *know* why she didn't complain about that. But the damned thing is named after me! Well, not literally named after me, but you know... You'd think she'd make the connection. I worked hard to set that up. You can't just do synchronicity all haphazard. Things need to connect. That connects. She's apparently on a space mission."

"Don't be too hard on her. Girl's had it pretty rough."

"I know that. It's what I'm trying to fix. What I *will* fix. One way or the other. But still, you get to haul Jakub off wherever the hell you guys want, and this one won't budge. Her head's like a lock box. I can't seem to get into it. It would help if I could present, but the timing and the energy are never right."

"Is she in a funk?"

"Off and on. I think she saw me when she went to Texas. I was in her hotel room, and it felt like she saw me there. Here, she turns the dials down low around this chick and I can't get anything accomplished."

"One day she'll be able to connect with you and find out just how awesome you are," Shelaine cooed. "It won't be like this forever. As long as she keeps working on her pet project, we're headed in the right direction."

"I don't think we have to worry about that. Girl's balls-to-the-wall on that one. You should see the diamond she picked up. It's not like a diamond-diamond, one of those crystal things that transmits energy. Herkimer?"

"Yeah, I know what you're talking about. I've heard of those. They collect the energy around them and kinda shoot it out like a radio signal."

"Exactly. She has those amethysts from that girl Veronica in a Faraday bag. But she charges that diamond every night. Been staying up late to do it. Think she's having them set tomorrow. I know she made a call for it, and she has an appointment."

"That'll be interesting to see, I mean, how that all works together."

"She's a pretty sharp cookie, that one. Hides it pretty well. She's good at playing dumb and playing dead. Sometimes I wonder if she thinks she has a possum for a totem animal."

Shelaine snorted and laughed, "That's *your* girl!"

"I meant it in the nicest possible way."

"So... you think this is gonna work? This plan the Lady has?"

"It'll work. We just all have to do our pieces and be patient. I know I have a hard time with that. It's heartbreaking to watch. I'd feel better if I could have a more interactive part in it, and that'll probably come soon, but for right now, it's like I have to watch her through a shop window and hope she does the right things. It can get absolutely maddening. She's just gonna have to learn how to be brave. To be something other than a survivor."

"She'll get there. I think all of these folks are gonna be different for the better once this is over with."

"You know what really rips at me? When she charges that diamond every night, she always says the same thing, and it breaks my heart to hear it."

"What's that?"

"Protect him and bring him back to me."

crawling back when

The grass was turning to dusty brown. She remembered the dying grass because no one was mowing their lawns anymore, at least that was how it appeared. School was a new year, her sophomore year, but the people were all the same, so she knew she could expect everything to be just as cold and distant as it had always been.

Billy Symons had begun talking to her at school, which was in itself a complete miracle. Amazingly, no one ostracized him like they did anyone else that had anything to do with her. He played baseball, and he was a junior.

Some of the abuse had subsided, people weren't talking about her and harassing her as much. Maybe things were finally beginning to change, and perhaps they had finally realized she wasn't any of the things they had been claiming her to be for years. She was finally beginning to get a little self-confidence back.

When he finally invited her over to his house, he'd said the family would be there, so she knew there wouldn't be anything necessarily romantic happening, but even at her age, she hadn't visited anyone else's house in years. Nor had she been invited to. It was still a special gesture for her, and she spent the next week fantasizing about it.

She walked. She lived a little over a mile away, and it made no sense to say anything to her mom because she was always too busy chatting with her friends down in Redondo. Dad was out of town working on the railroad gangs. He wouldn't be back until the following week.

Finding the house, she saw Billy smiling through the window. He waved her towards the back of the house, but he didn't open the front door.

As she rounded the corner into the backyard she saw Mindy Kreiser, the girl she had thought was his ex-girlfriend. Then his sister. Like ghosts, there were five of them circled around her.

This is about to go really bad.

"What you think you gonna find here, Spooky Girl? I bet I know what you'll find."

Running wasn't an option just yet, all of her escape paths were cut off. She prepared to run, placed her weight on her leg and pushed. It stopped her like she had ran into a brick wall.

She didn't know where the first blow came from, she felt it as she heard the yelling begin and as the panic began to engulf her, filling her body with a paralyzing sad electric, her brain was still trying to understand what had happened. It wasn't good. And Billy wasn't there.

Within three good hits, she was on the ground, trying to shield herself from the pain that was exploding through her body as every punch and kick landed on her until it was like swimming through mud. Her limbs didn't want to function, yet she tried to will herself to get away from what ever this was.

She started moving as a pain she had never felt before erupted on her scalp.

She was being dragged by her hair, waves of pain and heat mixing together in her brain. The beating hadn't stopped, but she couldn't fight, couldn't defend herself anymore.

Rolling didn't help. They acted as if she were a human soccer ball as she tried to change position, so would they, directing her in mud, through grass, and made sure she was located where the dog crapped.

The smell of meat. Burnt meat, and grease. The portable charcoal grill. They were dumping the ashes on her.

She felt the hands roughly pawing through her hair, pushing the ash and the grease into her once platinum blond hair and into her face. They were damaging her for the sake of damaging her, and the wild ecstatic joy they were getting from it was like a 200 pound demon sitting on her chest playing bongos to thrash metal.

At the corner of Billy's house stood Roger, laughing maniacally at the scene with his hand thrust in his pants. She felt the tug on her pants leg. They were trying to get her pants off of her, and that launched her panic into overdrive. She managed to latch her thumb into the belt loop and begged, holding it for dear life. At least they stopped trying to disrobe her.

The next kick got her in the face, and as she tried to recover from the needle pain from her nose and sinuses, she tasted the salt of her own blood mixed with the grease and the ash. She was hit in the head with the grill lid, heard it clang against the ground.

Water. The water was hitting the grass from a garden hose, and she was covered in the cold spray, saturating down to her skin. And then there was Billy. She could feel his presence. She was finally safe.

"Get in the house," he said to the girls as the violence subsided. "And somebody needs to tell that stupid scrawny bitch to get the fuck out of here. Mom's already called the cops on her. They'll come haul her off in a few minutes." There was no emotion in his voice. None of the kindness from before. No acknowledgment that she was even a human being he had ever known. He could have been talking about his dog. Or the trash.

She heard the door slam, and as swiftly as they had attacked, she was alone.

She felt like an animal. A wounded animal trying to escape the scene of a hunt. Anything that she knew as facts or figures had vacated the front of her mind, and she only knew one thing.

I don't want to die here.

Something superhuman came over her, and the tattered girl drove all of the pain and splintered pride into the center of her brain and rose to her feet, where she wobbled and teetered for a few steps until her body gained just enough strength to propel her away from this place. As she passed Roger, who was leaned against the house, he chuckled and said, "Well, *that* was delightful."

One foot in front of the other. She tried to not think as she let autopilot take over. One foot in front of the other. Don't think. Don't feel. Just move. Down to the sidewalk, over the railroad tracks. One more mile.

She could think later. Feel later. Analyze the damage she knew she was in, because if she did it now, the shock would stop her still and then it would all be over.

She reached the house, by some miracle was able to work the handle to get inside. Refused to look at herself in the glass on the door.

Her mother, still on the phone, took one disgusted look at her and said, "Well, look what the cat dragged in. What kind of trouble did you get into *this* time? Go clean yourself up and try to look presentable. What the fuck is that smell?" She then turned on a heel and left the room, still in her conversation on the phone.

The girl was alone. While it was typical, this was about the lowest it had ever been.

She stopped when she saw herself in the bathroom mirror. The lights made her eyes sting, but they were swelling and her nose was probably broken. The blood and ash and dirt looked as if she had been beaten and thrown into a coal mine. Everything vibrated flashes of pain in a rhythm, a drum beat from Hell itself.

As she tried to use a washcloth to get the filth off of her, wincing with every stroke. Her eyes lit on the sharp pair of scissors that had been stationed by the sink for some other purpose and forgotten.

One good stroke, and I'm out of this.

She grabbed the pair of scissors, her thumb and forefinger locked into the handle as if it were a weapon and retreated to a space next to the toilet, collapsing on her rear not knowing whether she was better off next to it or inside it. She didn't know how to do this.

Like a lamb goes to the slaughter...

The smell remained, clumps of hair stuck together in a paste of grease and charcoal, dog shit and mud. She spun the scissors around and began to cut, freeing lock after lock of soiled hair and dropping it. It could be cleaned up, but not now. Fuck everything. Not right now.

Fuck all of them.

When she finally felt the strength to stand again, she didn't recognize the girl in the mirror. She had no hair. She had no identity. And with the look in her eyes and the damage on her face, she had no soul.

She opened her laptop and turned on her webcam, her head splitting with every motion, every thought. Contacted the only person she thought would possibly help her anymore. It was a Hail Mary. As she saw the webcam connect on the other side, she had nothing she could say. The words wouldn't come. But she saw the woman's look of pain, of the horror of witnessing her in her new condition. That was all it took.

"*Fuck me, Lindsey.* I'm on my way, *beau bébé*. Just walk out when I get there. Leave *everything* behind."

It was the last day she was in that town, or in a school.

"That's why. That's why Lindsey has short hair." Veronica stood in shell shock. She looked in the moment like someone that was witnessing the carnage on a World War battlefield from the sidelines, the horror and majestic hatred of the moment sinking deep into her mind.

"Pretty much. That's all you have to say? Do you want to see more? There are years and years more of things like this, although this was probably the worst. Physically, anyway. She dealt with it until she could leave. You thought she had the perfect little life, because she was so pretty when you met her. How's it looking now?"

It was coming out much more caustically than she had intended.

Veronica had absolutely nothing to say. The Lady knew that there was really nothing she *could* say. It was horrific to watch that moment from the outside, unable to have any impact whatsoever, let alone be the one inside of it. It was a moment in history, and could not be undone.

She could sense the pain in the young girl, the empathy that she felt. This had hit hard because this was someone Veronica had known deeply in every way except romantically. Yet she'd never known about this dark secret. No one living except the ones there at the time knew of this. And of course one other person. Two if you counted Roger. But he wasn't an issue anymore. He was a problem that had found a solution.

She knew she was about to cut deeper, and it just had to be done because it was the truth.

"You can see now why she never connected to Hot Guy."

"Oh, you mean that guy she stalked for about six months?"

"She stalked him for over three years. Kinda still is. Because he is the only one she was ever meant to be with. The one that was going to take all of this hurt and pain away from her and help her heal. Getting those two together is just about impossible. They're maniacally in love with each other, yet mortally afraid of each other at the same time. It really screws up everything. Especially for me."

"So why can't they just get together?"

The Lady didn't want to, but she had to. This was going to be a kill point, but there was no other way to deliver it. Locking eyes with Veronica, she said, "They're having a hard time getting together because that jackass, for some reason I can only fathom, bought a used VR headset that you happened to be trapped inside of. So now, she's given him to you. Thinking of course that she's doing the right thing. For both of you. And to her, it feels like that," She said, pointing, "Like being beaten all over again."

The Lady waited a few moments to let it sink in. It did seem a bit cruel, but she knew that she'd have to break Veronica into reality in order to build her up again. There was more to this story that even Lindsey didn't know.

"I have something else to show you. I'm not saying it's right, but I'm not saying it was wrong, either. It just *was*. It was also never brought up or discussed. There was a reason Lindsey left town immediately. There was also a reason why her parents moved about a year after that."

They were standing near the same railroad track. It was dark, the middle of the night. A railroad maintenance pickup with the running lights visible came rolling down the rails. The truck slowed to a stop silently in front of the house she'd seen earlier, and the lights extinguished. They watched the figure in hunter's camouflage exit the driver's side, retrieve something bulky from the bed of the truck.

It was a compound bow. With a chubby hand, the clad figure pulled a bundle of arrows, each fitted with a cylindrical device taped to the shafts.

His breath flowed into the night from the cold like an angry elk as he lined them up quickly, the house lit by an adjacent streetlamp. The glint of the arrow blades shone faintly in the night like little light sticks. One by one the figure swiftly fired them with laser accuracy into the wall, through windows, into the front door. Gently he placed the bow back into the bed, and with a faint sound of metal on metal sped off down the track.

After 500 feet, he flipped the lights back on and rounded a corner. The light of noon changing the sky as the house burst into flames in the dark night with acrid smoke filling the air.

"My god," Veronica said, as they watched the building burn like a parcel of gasoline soaked twigs.

No one came out.

"Did they survive?" She asked.

"Huh? No, *no*..." The Lady answered. "None of them got out of that one."

"That's horrible," Veronica said, aghast.

"Really?" She asked the girl, "It's nothing Papa wouldn't have done. He would have just done it differently. How can you treat a person like they treated Lindsey and not expect retribution? Her mom might have been a bitch, but Daddy? He's a completely different animal. The sins of the son sometimes do rest on the father. Maybe that saying's backwards, but it certainly works in this case."

"How did Lindsey take this?"

"She didn't. You're the only one to ever see this. It was a crime that remains unsolved. I think it should stay that way. This wasn't a town with the brightest minds living in it. None of these people were going to design rockets or cure cancer. The arrows weren't out of place. They were overlooked. He had a year to think this out, and he's kept his mouth shut. Hester would have been proud. He's all about street justice. He had a pretty rough and dirty childhood, too."

"So I stole the best thing she ever had, after all this. I'm a really shitty friend."

"You still can't look at it that way. Think of it more like this," She paused, thinking, before addressing Veronica again, "Let's say that you and Lindsey are little toddler girls. Cute little things. You're best friends. You love each other. There is a juicy piece of caramel on the floor. She's been looking at it for the last fifteen minutes, thinking about how delicious it is. Her mommy dropped it on the floor. Yes, I know about her mother, but we're simulating here. Mommy drops the candy on the floor. You crawl around the corner, see the candy, you know what it is, so you pick it up and put it in your mouth. You don't even know she's seen it. She can't be mad because you picked it up and ate it. Well, she *can*, but we both know Lindsey won't."

"I still feel like shit."

"And yet you're still in love with him."

that particular color

"You should probably go with a lavender shirt. After all, you seemed to be a little attached to those, and they look pretty good on you. Get the French cuffs, like the shirt you had at OMB."

He knew the voice before he even turned to look.

"Where's Hester?" Jakub asked.

"He's handling some business with The Lady. Apparently she had to deal with your girl Veronica a little more roughly than she wanted to. She takes these things kinda hard, so..."

"So you're taking me clothes shopping. Where are we, anyway?"

"Seriously, dude? This is your old stomping grounds. How the hell do you not know Century City Mall?"

"Sorry. Been a minute since I was in LA. How's this gonna work, anyway? I can't buy clothing and take it home in a dream."

"No, but you *can* try things on and know what you're buying in a dream. Then you cart your sorry ass to the store and order the real thing. Chin up. We gotta get you all presentable."

"Why?"

"*Love is in the air*," Shelaine sang to him, "We'll start with the shirt, then figure out the rest. You have to look good. That's what matters."

"Where am I going?"

"Somewhere."

"And where is that somewhere?"

"Not here."

"You're not gonna tell me anything either, are you?"

"Welcome to the party. Shirts. We're looking at shirts." She called over an attendant who moved smooth as silk to where they were standing. "Hi, my friend here needs a dress shirt with French cuffs, preferably in a lavender tone. Do you have that?" The young man stopped to think, tapping his finger against his chin. It was almost the same move that Veronica used to do.

"Actually, yes. I *do* believe we have that. Were we thinking a solid, or are we looking for white trim?"

"*We* don't want our boy here to look like a bad stock broker or a pimp. So solid would be nice, yes."

"I can completely understand. In that case, I believe that stripes are out as well, which is very good because I find them most frightful."

"You are *my* kind of guy," Shelaine said. "And I should point out that we are researching today, not purchasing. That will happen in the next few days. Don't wanna get your hopes up too high there, since I know you work on commission."

"Understood." He showed no emotion, so it didn't seem to matter too much to him, but Jakub was pretty sure that it did. He withdrew a fabric tape, and with a few quick measurements stated cheerfully, "I believe I know what size we're looking for. Back in a moment."

As he sauntered off to the back, Jakub asked Shelaine, "Really... Why are we doing this again?"

"Because everyone needs a set of dress clothes... For special events."

"Do you have dress clothes?"

"I have a uniform with a lotta bling on it. Hester has more bling. That's better than a tuxedo, jack. So, yes. And you need something too."

The attendant returned with a beautiful purple dress shirt.

"At first, I was thinking maybe twill, but you seem to be the more refined type rather than a business type guy. Maybe I misread you, but that was what I picked up. So this is more of a soft, silk-like material." He was writing on a small pad. "You can try this on, and if you like it, I have the SKU here, and you can place it on order when you're ready." He turned to Shelaine and said, "Where else would we like to go from here, ma'am?"

She smiled gently at him and said, "We are going to need to go with a formal suit, something that would go along with what you've picked here. I'm very attracted to the style you're going with. We would want that in a black. Think red carpet, and we're probably going down the right avenue."

"Certainly. I have just the thing in mind," he said with a nod, as he backed away and returned to the back.

"My god," Shelaine said, "He's talking into my tits like they're a microphone."

"What did you expect? There's probably an online club of men that wished they could motorboat you."

"Yeah, I guess I get that a lot. At least we know what team *he* plays for now. Wait. Hey! Did you just say that shit to me?"

"Is it a lie?"

She exhaled. "Probably not. I guess I should count my blessings."

"You know Hess is."

She giggled. "I'm starting to like you more and more, kid."

"Seriously, you guys have been really good for me. I do appreciate everything. I have no idea what the hell is in front of me, but having you guys piloting the ship saves me a lot of blood pressure. I don't know what I'd do without you guys."

She gave him a serious look. "We think a lot of you, too. There's a lot gonna happen, and this is gonna get ugly, but we are both willing to give everything, including ourselves to get you where you gotta go. You have no clue how important you are just yet. We love ya like one of us. I just wish we could've thrown ya out of a plane one good time. That would have made it official."

"I could go skydiving."

"I don't care how many sky dives you get. Until you've jumped from 1250 feet into total darkness carrying 95 pounds of equipment with a 42 pound chute, to us, you're still a leg."

"That's kinda harsh."

"That's kinda the truth. Doesn't mean we love ya any less for being a leg. We all have faults."

The attendant returned with a sleek suit that appeared to almost be like a tuxedo. Shelaine took one look at it and said, "If it fits, it ships. That's beautiful work there. We like you. We're coming back to you next time."

"Thank you, ma'am."

"Let's get you dressed." She waited for him to get dressed. He felt awesome in that suit. It actually made him feel like he was somebody, which wasn't normal for him. He stepped out for Shelaine to survey him. Tried to blank out of his mind the fact that it was sometimes troublesome to have an advocate that was just, well, *damn.*

She flashed another grin that showed her teeth this time.

Dammit. I keep forgetting they can read my thoughts.

Turning to the attendant, she said, "What are we thinking for a tie?"

"Are we thinking a neck tie, or a bow tie?" the attendant stopped to look again. It was apparent that he was reconsidering.

"If it wouldn't be too avant-garde, might I suggest an inwrought tie? It's the best of both worlds, the up-and-down of the necktie, but the brevity of the bow tie. He'd look stylish without looking like a total nerd. It has class. Authority. Style."

"See? That's why I like working with you," Shelaine cooed. "I knew there was a reason I came to you today. That's perfect. Do you have one in stock?"

"Yes, yes I do. Deep purple, since that's the scheme we're going with." He disappeared, and quickly reappeared with a small item that appeared to be like a sideways bow tie. Jakub had to admit he'd never heard of an inwrought tie, but it was pretty badass.

"That," Shelaine said, looking almost in wonder, "Is a thing of *fucking beauty* right there." The attendant grinned for the first time.

"What shoes and belt would be required for this?"

"I think we can handle that part."

"Very well. Cufflinks?"

"Do you have purple butterflies? That part is very important. It's almost non-negotiable."

"I don't believe we would have those. I would try online, or maybe Bloomy's."

"If you don't have it, I doubt they will. It is kinda an off-market thing."

Turning to Jakub, Shelaine asked, "So what do ya think, champ?"

"I think it's an incredible look. No idea what I'm wearing it to, but it looks *really* damned good."

"Spectacular!" She answered. Looking at the attendant, she asked, "Do you have that list of SKUs?" She turned to Jakub and said, "It looks absolutely smashing on you, but I think they need their clothes back now. Temporarily, of course." Jakub went back to change. The attendant was still verifying everything when he returned with the clothes. He'd tried to re-fold them the way he'd gotten them. He wasn't sure he'd done it right.

"Yes, ma'am, here it is." The attendant gently tore the page from the pad and handed it to her.

Shelaine handed it back and said, "We need your name. Want you to get credit for all of your hard work, of course. Wouldn't be right to do it any other way."

"Ah, yes ma'am. I apologize. I'm Claude. I'm sorry. I think I might have forgotten to mention that before."

"No worries. You have been absolutely wonderful today, and when we purchase, we'll make sure to let your management know just how helpful and knowledgeable you've been today."

"Thank you, ma'am." He nodded and with a smile took his leave.

As they walked out into the sunshine, Jakub couldn't resist one last prod.

"So you're not going to tell me what event we're going to?"

"Not a chance in Hell. But I promise you, this will be sweeter than the most perfect dessert you have ever put in your mouth." She slightly turned her head to the side and said, "Is that a L'Occitane? We're making a pit stop. Hess owes me."

When it ends

"This is all just getting to be too damned much," Jakub said to him. They were seated at the Statesman, Jakub with his usual, and Aiden sampling one of the local microbrews Austin was becoming famous for.

"I mean, I get the whole 'traveling in your dreams' part, but this is just ridiculous. I actually tried on a suit in my sleep last night."

"There are many people that can say that when they're awake," Aiden responded, taking a long drink from his bottle.

"And this isn't weird to you?"

"In the right city, under the right circumstances, everybody's fucked up, and you have to realize you're the only one who isn't. So none of this is strange to me anymore. This is tame to what you see once you leave the country. The first time someone gets bent because you don't want their roasted rat on a stick, you realize that the world is somewhat bizarre. Buying clothes in your sleep is tame. Drunk shopping is worse, especially online. SWI. Shopping While Intoxicated is how most people get tattoos."

"Ah, I have a tattoo story for ya, but you hafta know the guy for it to be funny, I guess."

"Probably. Hey, wait!" He blurted, giving a friendly wave to Stefan, "Could I trouble you for a 512 Pecan Porter?"

Stefan nodded, "Ya in the right place for that one. I'll bring it in just a sec." Looking along the bar, he saw a polished wooden box and a placard that read IN MEMORY OF, but he couldn't read the name. It had a photograph framed of a man with a goatee, a glazed smile on his face raising a cocktail glass. He'd apparently had one too many there.

When Stefan returned and gently sat his beer on the table, Aiden gestured and asked, "To whom do we owe the honors over there?"

"Ah, ask your buddy about him. That's Garry Hollister. He used to be a regular patron. Died right outside when he walked in front of a oncoming truck. Sad story. But Jakub with a 'u' here, and his friend helped the guy out, from what I understand. I just know that nothing creepy has been happening in here since. Whatever they did, it worked. He ain't here now. Fat Man thought it would be a good tribute to put him out there like that. I know I don't have a problem with it."

"That's cool then." Raising his glass, Aiden announced, "To Garry, God rest his soul!"

Stefan smiled. It was a feat. He wasn't the most cheerful guy to walk the planet, so a moment of mirth on his face was an achievement. Usually he was bitching about something, and most of the time it was his boss that he called the Fat Man. Aiden wasn't sure if that was exactly affectionate or not. It was probably just affectionate enough to keep him from being fired.

After Stefan ambled off, Jakub looked over and asked, "Have you given any more thought to that energy healing thing you were talking about?"

"I've certainly given thought to that cute girl." He saw that Jakub wasn't joking. "I *have* given it thought. I'm not quite sure where I'm gonna go with it, or who it will be with, but it won't be in Colorado. I know better than to try it that way. When I say I'd never be able to learn anything under her, I mean it. She's too pretty for me, and I wouldn't hear a word she was saying. I'd be spending all my time having sexual fantasies about her. So that won't work. I hafta come up with something else. But yes, I think it's gonna be a thing."

"Good. I think that with all the energy you give off, it'd be a really positive thing for you and everybody else. It would really suit you. You're the kinda guy that would make a good healer because people just gravitate towards you almost uncontrollably, and if you had something even more useful to give back, that's great for everybody."

"Wow," Aiden held back slightly surprised. "That's a really nice thing you said right there. You really think people 'gravitate' towards me?"

"Uh, you're joking, right? Any time we go anywhere, except here, of course, people are always coming up and talking to you first. When you talk, people stop and listen. You're such a interesting guy you could star in your own beer commercials."

"Do I hafta pick a beer yet?"

"Not yet, buddy. You got time."

"So what about your deal? What about this mentor, teacher, whatever that I never get to see?"

"I guess you're never at the right place at the right time."

"Well, dish out. Tell me about her."

"She's pretty. I know that's what you're asking. You're wanting to know if she could make it into the *Grand Book of Hotties Aiden Stares At*, and yes, she could. I don't have the luxury of looking at her that way, but I think you two could hit it off. And it wouldn't really bother me, just remember that she still has to teach me a lot of this weird shit that's going on around me now."

"I think I can stay outta the way of that. But I'd need her every few nights for routine maintenance."

"Whoa there, tiger. You haven't even met the woman yet."

"Don't have to. You said she made it into the Hottie book. I trust your judgement. Maybe she'll be so awesome that she'll knock me out and drag me by the hair to her cave. Then you'll need that suit you were tryin' on. Okay. Enough jerkin' around. Tell me more."

"Well, she's kinda quiet, and it doesn't seem to me like she's dated anyone in a while, like she seems to have taken herself off the market. Don't know why. Don't know if she'll talk about it. Seems almost like she's damaged goods or something."

"Well, we're all damaged goods in some way or another, I reckon."

"Reckon? You're getting more Texan by the day."

"Yeah, and I'm proud of it, too."

"I'm damn glad to have infected you with the Lone Star Virus then. That'll suit ya too. Big and friendly. Like a Saint Bernard."

"Those are Swiss," Aiden clarified.

"They like mountains. You like mountains. You like ski bunnies. I think it rather suits you. And yes, if the moment presents itself, I'll make sure you two meet."

"You are a bro," Aiden said gratefully.

"Don't thank me yet. It hasn't happened. Why are you even looking for women like that anyway?"

"I don't know. I haven't thought about it. I usually don't. I like to go with the flow of things and just see what happens. That's part of the whole adventure, right?"

"Life is not a Choose Your Own Adventure book."

"Bullshit. It is, too. That's *exactly* what it is. It also has sections that are not meant for children, and that's the sections I'm interested in right now."

"Son, you just won't do. Those are the sections that *result* in children." Jakub said with a smile. "So, you've been drinking..."

"I'm gonna keep drinking."

"What's this event I'm supposed to be getting ready for?"

"I ain't ever gonna be *that* drunk. You make a mean brisket, but I ain't givin' up those carnitas. Nor will I endure the ass-whoopin' that would be invested unto me if I were to divulge even the tiniest smidge of information. No wine, women, *or* song will make me cough up that one."

"Fair enough. I guess I'll find out on my own."

"That's an understatement."

"What?"

"Just trust everybody. Nothing bad is gonna happen to you. In fact, it should be one of the best moments of your life. Let's just say that something's coming, and that something's gonna have you so busy thanking everybody that you're gonna forget about all the suspense."

"I sure hope so."

"I *know* so. So why aren't you dating? Seriously. It's an honest question."

"The girl I love is dead."

"She ain't the only girl on the planet, though. I'm not trying to be a heartless dick, I'm just saying, you're the kinda guy somebody out there deserves."

"There is only one other girl out there on the face of the Earth that could get my attention, and she doesn't want my attention. So in that case, the bar's closed. Everybody's been kicked out on their ass, and they're washin' the dishes."

"Only one, huh? Okay. I'll play your stupid game. What if that 'other girl out there on the face of the Earth' decided that she *did* want your attention? Like, wanted it a lot. 'Me love you long time' a lot? What about that?"

The look on Jakub's face was nothing short of miserable.

"The thought of that being a possibility hasn't really crossed my mind. It's a fantasy, at best. And believe me, I've had a *lot* of fantasies about that girl. But I know what the reality is, and I've accepted that it won't happen."

"Shit," Aiden said, exhaling. "I guess I hit below the belt there. Sorry about that. Maybe things change. Anything's possible."

in other life

"Everyone loves you. It doesn't matter if they were a guy or a girl, you can have anyone you want. You're like Helen of Troy."

Lindsey was hearing these words from the mouth of Veronica, who still had puffy cheeks from crying. They stuck with her, haunted her. They had bounced around in her head for the past three and a half years, pricked and poked the inside of her brain with little needle-like incisions.

Because they were untrue.

In the moment, Veronica was making a comparison. It was true that she'd had to build a really tough shell from all the men constantly vying for her attention. Having a girlfriend had reduced that to a point, but then opened a whole new package of people that were also trying to get her attention.

She didn't *want* their fucking attention.

Because there was a time when no one wanted her attention. In fact, they brought the focus to her so she could be crushed like a bug, humiliated, so they could see her cry, and then that was a big joke, too. Those scars were fault lines that ran deep in her soul, they never seemed to heal up and smooth over.

One of the first things she'd dealt with, after Lindsey had told her friend in desperation about Roger, was her friend proving not to be so much of a confidante. The girl spread the talk about her seeing dead people, and that escalated and twisted to weird séances and Ouija boards and demons. All sorts of nonsense that had never been discussed. Another rumor said she was a witch, and in that little backwoods religious town, that went horribly wrong as well.

Some kid had formulated a bad joke, and soon people she didn't even know were calling her "*The Linzercist*". It was a silly mock-up of *The Exorcist*, but no one cared about the fact that an exorcist throws out demons, they aren't possessed by them. She seemed to be the only one that didn't think it was funny.

Three years later she was still pulling down photos of Linda Blair in her iconic role from out of her locker. Twice she had to clean up green children's play goo from the bottom of it. The teachers and staff were every bit as culpable as the kids actively torturing her, and nothing was done about it in the least.

God help her around Halloween.

Another time there was a can of split green pea soup with a note, "Don't forget this!" attached. Her mother was useless. Her response was always something along the lines of "If you hadn't opened your mouth, there wouldn't be anything to make fun of, would there?"

No mercy, no assistance, no defense.

Dating for Lindsey was non-existent. Amazing as it was to anyone that knew her now. But in all her years, she'd never went or been invited to a middle school dance, high school homecoming, was never invited to a prom. Somewhere in the beginning of her freshman year, her classmates doubled down on the rumor mill, and it being a small town in the middle of the state, she was probably just lucky that they didn't burn her at the stake.

To even consider having friendly conversations with "the spooky girl" would have sullied the offending party's reputation, and there would have been hell to pay.

She had learned to speak only when it was absolutely necessary, which added to the abuse. Lindsey went from the crazy girl who played with dead people and the devil to a wannabe nun that wouldn't put out.

She was 16 when that day happened. Trying to keep it out of her mind only worked some of the time. But there had been Jeanette, lovely Aunt Jeanette, and Lindsey couldn't get out of that town fast enough.

She never went back.

Her parents finally moved because Daddy had made headway with the railroad and with the new prosperity, they relocated closer to Los Angeles and the beach. They never fully understood why Lindsey rarely came around. Maybe her father knew. He wouldn't discuss it. He wouldn't talk about *any* of it.

But Aunt Jeanette was crystal clear on the issue. It had been her house that Lindsey had gone to in her worst moments, and she had to be the mother figure when her sister wouldn't. Aunt Jeanette had known what it was like to be an oddball and an outcast, but she admittedly had never been forced to face down the humiliation and abuse that Lindsey had.

"There's a purpose to this, I promise you," she would say to her as she held her in her arms and stroked her hair, "You are meant for a grand design. No one suffers without a higher purpose. They just can't always see it."

Jeanette was right. She couldn't.

But she did know that doing something stupid wasn't the answer, and by stupid, she meant self-destructive. *Every puzzle has its solution, and every maze has an exit.* That was something that Veronica had always said, and she proved it too. When she wasn't working on something or talking to Lindsey, she was working puzzles. Veronica was particular to logic problems and Sudoku. She could spend hours working them out, and hated to leave one unfinished. For her, it was like not feeding the rabbit.

Luna.

Lindsey knew why the rabbit was so important, and why it was so important to give one to Jakub. That was something that was sacred and special. She wasn't particularly fond of the smells it gave off sometimes, but that soft fur and gentle disposition just made everything forgiven.

Never in a million years had she suspected that she would be here, with Veronica gone, and that she would be doing this for Jakub. It had been a gargantuan effort, and Lindsey had certainly pulled off much more than she'd suspected she would have been capable of, all of it under the radar.

She was in a complete panic about how all of this was going to be received. Willie seemed to think it was a great idea, and she knew she was yet again foolishly hanging her hopes on another person's opinion.

Veronica was the only one other than her Aunt Jeanette that had known about Roger, the only one that knew about the green bear that had hosted him. So when Jakub came in on that day and brought it up, she knew that there was something serious and horrific at foot.

It was a sisterhood thing. Neither of them had a sister, so they had become sisters by proxy. It was a bond that she still held deep. She felt guilty that she was still as much in love with Jakub as she'd been as a courier, stalking him like he was the only boy on Earth.

Here she was about to hand him over yet again. Every time she thought she might get close, the carrot got pulled out further. Sometimes she felt like a rabbit herself. More like the one that was skinned and eaten, and less like the cartoon rabbit.

She had a friend she couldn't see or talk to, and she was always just out of reach. Hell, she didn't even know exactly who she was, and that had been the great puzzle as of late, figuring out who this person was, if they had a name, where she'd even come from.

It was her name she couldn't remember. She was somebody important, but Lindsey couldn't seem to recall how. Maybe it was something in a dream. Started with a 'C'. She knew because she'd seen it written down somewhere and recalled that it was important. Someone she was very attracted to, felt comfortable with. Almost like a lover, but not. It was someone that cared about her.

A woman. She knew that much.

Celeste? No. That wasn't it. She couldn't seem to visualize her, either, even though she knew she'd seen her somewhere.

Maybe it was something more Greek, or French. Lindsey couldn't quite decide. But she knew it was a name that was in front of her face a lot. The symbols at the convention center had meant "Call Me". The angel girl in the dream that blew Roger apart had said the name, too. But she remembered the cacophony more than the content of what was said.

Chairs. She kept pointing at chairs. Maybe a name of someone that sat in a chair.

Caroline? Catherine? Neither of them were exotic. That wasn't right. But she could feel it deep within her, and Lindsey knew if she were able to forget it and just relax, it would come to her.

The coffee on her side table had begun to cool, and she watched a skin of cocoa form on the top. It always seemed like the best parts of things solidified and rose to the top. Then they stuck to you no matter how you wanted to have them gone, or wanted to enjoy them. Love was basically like the scum on top of a cooling coffee.

I'm not gonna win any literature awards with that one.

misplaced

"How do you *really* feel about Lindsey. What is the truth?"

"I love her. I love her like a sister. I'd trust that girl with my life."

"Then do it."

"What do you mean by that? What am I missing?"

"Look, here's how it's going to end up shaking out," The Lady said, "I know how you feel about him. I get it. Believe me. Jakub's gonna have a lot to figure out, and he isn't really going to be able to do that for a while. He's on a road back home, and it will be rough. Look at it from my side. I have two women that knew him in life. Both of them love him deeply. He was only supposed to have one or the other. Now he has both. Because of how you two met, the game just changed."

"What do you mean 'changed'? How did it change?"

"He's now putting one foot solidly in our realm. It's a gateway that has to be protected at all costs.

He needs the love of someone he trusts while he's incarnate, and you know that can't be you. He also has another specific task to complete before he can come back here. But when it's completed, he will be back here, with you. He has you from this side. You are going to learn a lot soon on how to accomplish that. You'll be able to help a great deal, find new ways to interact with him. But I have to warn you. After you go through Induction, the *way* you love him is going to change."

Veronica didn't like the way this conversation was going. Some contact was better than no contact, and whatever this was with Lindsey, well, she'd rather it be her than anyone else, especially now that she knew that Jakub was her Hot Guy that she'd been obsessed with and could have almost told you what brand of toilet paper he used.

For as many tears as she'd shed over all her failed relationships, Lindsey had cried twice as many tormenting herself over her target. It made a lot more sense.

She was wondering exactly what she'd gotten herself into. They said she was connected to this Lady, but she couldn't imagine how. She did look a lot like Mama, though. But she wasn't Avo or Granny. So that wasn't it.

"Can I ask a question?"

"Sure, Baby Girl."

"How are we connected? I mean you and I, how do we fit together?"

"I was your advocate."

"No, there's something more than that. You look like Mama."

"I would certainly hope so."

"But you don't fit anyone that I know."

The Lady smiled at her and paused. "You don't realize who I am, then."

"No, I don't. Like I said, you don't fit anyone I know."

"Then I think that's a secret I need to hold onto for a little longer. It will all come out when it needs to."

"So what is this Induction you were talking about?"

"It's a form of conditioning that sets you better on our side. You need to understand that there's no procreation here. Those are extra emotions, extra sensations that belong to the incarnate. That's why you are feeling and having to fight with these waves of jealousy. Don't try to hide them, they are perfectly natural, and they won't fade until you are through Induction. You'll still love Jakub, that will not get taken away. But it's gonna go even *deeper* than you ever imagined, and you'll have even more information than you ever knew possible, see things you didn't think you could get to afterwards."

At least that was a bit reassuring.

"Can I make it simple?"

"God. Please do."

"The day will come when she'll love him when he's awake, and you'll love him when he's asleep. Love is not just sex. I know that's what it's all about there in that place, but it isn't the solid material love is made of. It's deeper, thicker, more complete. His soul needs to be fed. I would like to think that he has a very exemplary support system being put in place. After all, we have functions that we both have to perform." She paused and seemed to glaze for a moment.

"Have you ever watched a women's roller derby?" She asked.

"Yeah, they had it on TV when I was a kid. I think Papa used to watch it," Veronica responded.

"Okay, so you know what a whip is? One person grabs another teammates' arm and flings them forward?"

"Yeah. I've seen that."

"That's what's happening."

"I don't get it. Who's 'we'?"

She grew quiet, seeming to battle within herself for the next words she was going to say.

"Jakub and I are connected. You and I are connected. Lindsey is connected to all of us. This whole interaction thing is part of the *Wilwarin Nosse*. In time, you'll understand what is going on here, why everything seems to be so intense."

"Sometimes, I wish it wasn't. It's tiring, and I never know where I'm at in anything. One minute I feel like I'm on top of the world, and then in the next I'm back to the bottom of the barrel again. Does it ever get normal, am I gonna ever get any relief on this?"

The Lady smiled at her and said, "Yes, the time is coming when everything will be just fine. You'll be full, and your heart will be at peace. And when he comes back and you retrieve him, it will be a beautiful day. Good things are coming, but some of the hard things need to come first. Now you have to be a spectator until he can reach through the veil."

It made her feel a little better. It was nice to know that somewhere there was good coming of this, a point where her heart wouldn't hurt so bad, where she wouldn't feel like she'd lost out on everything.

"You'll begin to feel more outside of yourself. And what I mean by that is more of an empathic nature. Like I can feel what you're feeling right now, and that is why I try to make sure that what I'm telling you matches or corrects the emotion you're having. One day you'll be able to feel that out and do the same thing. So you're going to develop and learn, become better here. I know you're all about that sort of thing."

"So that's why you always seem to have the right thing to say."

"It is. And one day you will do the same thing for Jakub. But you have to remember, He has serious work to do while he's incarnate. That work gets him back here, but you'll have to be patient. To be honest, we'll *both* need to be patient, because I have a vested interest in this as well."

"You have an interest in this?"

She acted confused at the question. "Of course I do. This stuff doesn't magically happen! There's a lot of planning and scheduling involved. Everybody's supposed to be in the right place at the right time, otherwise everything gets all off track and adjustments have to be made, like what we're doing now. Had it all went according to plan, Jakub would already be over here again. So he's late. He's on borrowed time."

"Wait, so you're saying that if he had connected with Lindsey the first time..."

"Yes, he would have already passed and would be here right now."

"And I would have never met him. At all."

"Correct." She reconsidered and relented, "Well..."

Veronica shook her head, "But that would have been *no bueno*. So why was it that we did meet? How did I get put into that mix?"

"Because you're connected to *me*, Baby Girl. I requested it myself."

"And *how* am I connected to you? You haven't told me that yet."

"Because it isn't germane right now. You don't need to know how we're connected. Just know and be happy that we are. I know I'm grateful for it, and I've been grateful to be with you most of the minutes of your incarnation. It's a good thing. I promise."

"Can you tell me about Mama? How long will she be there?"

The reaction was different. The sadness was on her face, and it wasn't a usual thing to see.

"Mama will be fine. She has many more years left, and although she's had a lot of pain, she will soon be in Jakub's corner as well. It'll be like having another son for her, and that's good. She is healing. She's done very well, given her circumstances."

"So she's connecting with Jakub?"

"Yes, eventually. And that's good. You should find some happiness in that."

"I do."

"I should admit, because it's only fair, that I will love Jakub more than any of you ever could. And he will love me more deeply than he can ever love any other sentient or energetic being other than The Source."

Veronica felt like she had just been crumpled up like a used paper cup.

"No, you don't understand, Baby Girl," She said, reaching out and running her fingers through

Veronica's hair, "Cyanophrys, that's his real name, is my *onona*. We're twins."

on the ground

When Willie thought about what was coming, she felt excited. The problem was that she had a hard time keeping a secret. But this one required it, and she was proud of herself for actually being able to carry it out. Only the right people knew the things they needed to know, and she put special effort into trying to make sure everything Lindsey had talked about would go according to plan.

And Lindsey was such a beautiful girl, too. That was the part that made it so sad. Willie had adored Veronica, but she'd never actually met her in the flesh. She just had pictures, the video from Jakub's apartment, and his stories.

Lindsey was perfect. A completely hot mess broken perfect, but perfect. She was beautiful, soft, gentle, and yet somehow when that girl looked in the mirror, she didn't see what everyone else saw in her. That was the part that made Willie mad. She knew first hand what abuse and injustice like that looked like from the antics of their mother, and manipulation just made her angrier.

She was proud that Jakub had not picked that up. He was just a decent guy all around. What she had kept hidden from Lindsey was the fact that those years Jakub spent mostly drunk was because of *her*. What he thought was his inability to get the time of day from Lindsey, for some reason Willie could not get out of him, had led to a drinking habit that wasn't solved by money or relationships.

It was true that he'd stopped drinking because of Veronica, and that was sacred ground that Willie wouldn't dare cross. To Willie, it still staggered the mind that those two had been best friends and lived together, yet neither had known the other was attracted to the same guy or that they had known him.

Okay, so Lindsey had known, but she had been in no place to say or do anything, and Veronica hadn't really known. This was all a nice chaos clusterfuck.

"What's chewin' on ya, babe?" Carl asked. He always knew when she was in deep processing mode. For all the faux hell she gave them, her family was the best thing she had in her life. Carl was certainly the best thing that had happened for her. He'd put up with a lot of shit to get her out of dodge, and remained the buffer that kept Willie from going to Houston and beating the piss out of her mother with a lead pipe on a regular basis.

"Thinking about this whole Lindsey thing."

"Jakub's girl?"

"Veronica is Jakub's girl."

Carl snorted.

"Look, babe," He began, "You can't bullshit a bullshitter. I happen to own a dick, even if you keep it in your shed most of the time. You can lead a horse to water, but you can't make him drink. And I ain't stupid. You know as well as I do that even though we ain't said shit about him hauling that toy rabbit around, that if he had even the slightest clue that Lindsey was about him, finally, after all these years, he wouldn't just be drinkin' the water, he'd be rollin' and wallerin' in that stream like a pig in shit."

"Well, that's a romantic way to put it."

"I'm not designed for that flow'ry stuff. You know that."

"It's what she's doing that blows my mind. To have that much love for someone that doesn't even know it, and to have that very same person just as madly in love with you, and then she's going to let go without either of them knowing what's up? It's criminal. Absolutely criminal. I wanna lock 'em in a room together for a week like mating dogs and not let 'em out till something fun happens."

"But do ya really wanna get in the middle of that?" Carl asked, almost pleading.

"I *am* in the middle of that!" Willie exclaimed, exasperated. "I'm in a position where I just don't think I can let this one slip. I mean, picture it. Someone you know and care about is comin' to a fork in the road. He goes right, everything's sunshine, roses, and fuckin' unicorns. He goes left, he gets a one way, all expenses paid trip off a cliff. Which would you want?"

"You said all expenses were paid?"

"Be serious."

"I am being serious. You people keep me a very broke man."

"Broke is better than broken, which is what you'll be if you don't get serious."

"Depends on what you're breakin'. I know something you can break after the kids go to bed." It was obvious he saw the look on her face, because Carl saved himself. "Okay, okay. I get it. Of course you want him to go the right direction. We all do. He's been through enough pain, and from what you've told me about that girl, she has too. They both deserve something good, even if they are both too much in the wind to do it themselves. I agree. Sometimes extreme measures have to be taken. You've done a lot on this, and been really good at keeping it away from Jakub. To his credit, I doubt Aiden's gonna give him an inch or an inklin' on what this is all about. He's good like that. He sees what this is, too. I'm really glad those two stumbled on each other. I think they both needed a good friend."

"Yeah, that's a great thing. But I still just feel like there's more I can do to make this other wrong, right. He needs someone to snuggle up against when he's cold."

"No, that's you. Women are the ones that need to snuggle up against things. Men have the sense to buy another blanket."

"Quit bein' a dick. I'm serious."

"I am, too. And I agree. Aiden's been good, and someone to talk to other than that fish, as awesome as it is. But having a woman around that you care about, that just makes everything worth it. Nothing else is really that important if you have that."

"Now *that* was romantic. You're improving."

"Well, you can at least help deal with all the paperwork that's involved. There was a lot there that maybe no one else really knew how to do or even could do, and you're able to fix that."

"And that fucking cunt Sarah," Willie spat.

"Whatever you do, don't hit her. Please don't hit her. We don't need a scene, and once you get pissed, you'd plow through her like a fricking pit bull. Speaking of which, I ain't gonna take the blame if you latch on her ankle and don't let go. I know you," Carl said.

"You can't do that shit to people. That's abuse up front. And to just think of all the time they lost because of her shit."

"Willie, sweetheart, you know as well as I do that everthin' comes out in the wash. She'll get hers. When push comes to shove, she'll get hers. Just like yer momma's eventually gonna get *her* payday."

"You can't blame me givin' it a little push then, can ya?"

"I would know better than to try and take that away from you."

"I have a better idea."

"Do I even wanna know?" Carl asked, weakly. Carl always seemed to know when her light bulb went off, and he was a smart enough man to clear out of the way when that happened.

Willie grinned wickedly, "Honey, it's probably gonna be better if you didn't. Let's just say I'm gonna kill two birds with one stone, and one of those birds needed to get roasted anyway."

"Sounds like a chef's job."

"I'm definitely cookin' somethin', I promise ya that. We'll just hafta be patient while it's in the oven."

wasted breaths

Everything was now in order, but she was trying to figure out why she'd even done it.

She dialed and waited for the answer, wondering why she had never done so before. There was chance after chance, but she'd been so self-conscious about it, the feeling of being cussed out or hearing the words she had never wanted to hear.

Still ringing. Please don't dump me to voicemail.

Lindsey was still begging, pleading in her mind when Jakub's voice came alive in the speaker.

"Hi. Who is this?" He asked.

"Lindsey. Don't you recognize the number?"

"I've never *had* your number."

That struck her as strange.

"Whaddaya mean, you never had my number? Sure you did. I gave it to Sarah to give you a *long* time ago, like back when I was running courier."

"Um, when was this?" Jakub asked, "I asked for your number the first time I saw y'all talking, and she told me that I couldn't have it because you liked girls and you two were dating."

"*Really.*"

"Really. I asked Sarah, she said you didn't want me to have it. I've always thought you hated me. You didn't have two words to say to me until Veronica. I still have no idea what the hell I ever did."

Lindsey felt like she had Styrofoam in her throat. Something about this conversation was not going right. There were serious implications if he was telling her the truth. She was pretty sure that he was.

"Why would you think I hated you?" She asked Jakub, "What led you to that conclusion?"

"Uh, Sarah made it really damned clear. She said you, and I quote, 'couldn't stand my ass' and that I was 'too emo and pathetic in the first place', even though I've never been classified as 'emo' in my life. I have emails to prove it. I have it in *print*. I think I also have the one about being disgusted by me and I probably had a needle dick. Which was kinda out of bounds, because neither of you have ever seen me with my pants off, or I mighta went to jail."

"I think we have a serious problem goin' on here, then. Because I've never said anything about you to Sarah, other than ask her to give you my number back when you were at McT & K. And we didn't become a thing until after you left. In fact, that's kinda *how* we became a thing."

"Wait, what? You did what?"

"I asked her to give you my number. You wouldn't take it. Or so she said. I think I'm getting a good idea of what got played, and I'm starting to get a little pissed."

"A little? I'm a *lot* pissed. She always made it sound like she was my best friend and she had to fight you to be around me. I always wanted to be around you, not her."

"I have to figure out how I'm gonna deal with this. I don't completely know what, but something has to be done. After all, I had to hunt down Willie like a professional to get to you."

"Whaddaya mean 'hunt down'?"

"I had to hunt her down. Get the number, call. I flew out here a couple weeks ago and met her."

She heard the line go silent.

"You're the one she was talking about. I couldn't get anything else out of her. I'm humbled you went to those lengths for *me*."

Boy, you have no idea the lengths I'll go to.

"Well, ya gotta do what ya gotta do."

"You flew out to Texas for me, and you had the balls to take on Willie. Will wonders never cease?"

"Willie's a sweetheart. She acted almost like she was my sister."

"Then you made a damned good first impression. If she has any misgivings about ya, she'll cut through you like a hot knife through butter. Leave ya an oily mess on the floor."

"Hmm. She actually hugged me."

"You are in her majesty's good graces then. Did she bring the kids along?"

"No. I haven't met them."

"Then that's next, I promise you. That's the next test for Marion Ravenwood. Endure the wild free-range children."

"Who?"

"Marion Ravenwood. Y'know, the angry girlfriend from *Raiders of the Lost Ark*?"

"So I'm the girlfriend of Indiana Jones now?"

"Position's open." Sounded like a slight hiccup, "I should just shut up now. This conversation always went better in my head."

"I always wondered why I was so driven to do all of this. I think it's getting a bit clearer for me now. So here's where the conversation's gonna get weirder than it already is."

"Yeah? How so?" Jakub asked.

"Okay, so I know what Jeanette did, and I know that you're gonna start seeing dead people, if you haven't already, but has anything extra started happening?"

"What do you mean by 'extra'?"

"Like, *extra*. Not really ghosts or spirits, at least how we'd think of them. I saw these two girls at the Dallas Airport. One of 'em kinda looked like Veronica's mom, but it wasn't her because she's very much alive. The other one has reddish hair, cut down into a buzzcut. Really pretty face."

"And tattoos."

"What?"

"She has tattoos. Her right arm is tattooed down to the knuckles, and there's a lotus on her wrist. On her left leg there's a butterfly on her shin."

"How do you know that?" Lindsey asked with a gasp.

"Well, my advocates have been taking me on these weird trips, and the first one was to a hotel in Serbia. That's where I saw that girl. She's an advocate too. Worked on my Life Plan some way."

"Wild. That sounds exactly like her. I had a guy come up to me when I was working the convention center and tell me that she was right behind me. Then after I met Willie, I saw her again in my hotel room."

"What does Sarah think about that?"

"I'm not telling her anything about that. I'd never hear the end of it. We're honestly in a less than pleasant situationship more than anything else. It was even that way when you lived in LA. She'd have me locked up so she could hunt a new girlfriend. Probably is anyway. If it's not already part of the ongoing discussion she wants to have, or directly related in some way, she's tuned to a dead station. I could talk to Veronica all day about that stuff, but not her. I don't really even talk to her about much anymore unless I have to."

"Sounds like you need to get out of that and get on your own."

"I don't make anything like the kinds of money Sarah makes as a paralegal, and she makes damned sure I know it, too. I don't know if I could sustain myself on my own. She certainly doesn't think so."

"I think you could pretty much do anything you set your mind out to do, at least that's the way you've always struck me. Look, if you need help, there will always be love for ya out here."

"That was what Willie said, almost exactly. And I think I will probably start putting some ideas into motion. Let's just keep the Sarah thing on ice for right now. We'll have a go at her later. In the meantime, you have an event to attend tomorrow."

"I do?"

"Yep. That's really why I called in the first place, but I think the event has slightly evolved since I first envisioned it. That's okay. You'll see what I mean."

"Where is it? What is it?"

"So, I'm about to text you some coordinates, and here are your instructions. You're gonna call in sick to work tomorrow and take a personal day. Do it first thing, because you're gonna want to get on the road early. Wear the best suit you own."

"Wait, dress up?"

"Uh, yeah. This is kinda a big thing. Dress up."

lavender and sand

The GPS coordinates led him to a place he was not quite expecting. Mission San Jose was the intended destination he had been provided, and Jakub felt strange going there in a suit on a Thursday morning.

As he walked the narrow walkway into the mission, he surveyed the ornate entrance of crumbled sand colored stone, the carvings still intact over the frame. Something just felt *holy* about the place.

He had been here before in the past, as a tourist, and remembered some of the history that was in this place. Grasping at mental facts and figures from an experience so far removed from where he was now, he knew that these missions were the places that Ronni had seemed to love with passion. She had talked about them in vivid detail and there was one place that she had loved the most.

Entering into the wide courtyard in the middle of the mission, he saw off to his left a crowd of well-dressed people near a smaller fenced off entrance and wondered what this was Lindsey had gotten him into.

A woman in a lavender off the shoulder dress was headed his way, at a clipped pace. Jakub was stunned to recognize that the woman was Lindsey herself. She was absolutely radiant and looking like she had strolled off yet another magazine cover, perhaps this time a bridal magazine as a maid of honor. She didn't give the chance to respond, as Jakub tried with everything he had to not float away in her eyes.

With a wide smile she gently chided, "Hurry up! You're gonna be late to your own wedding!"

"Excuse me?"

She linked an arm with his and said, "Look, you're the groom. Thanks to Willie, we've set up a wedding by proxy. The paperwork says you're marrying Veronica, but that priest thinks you're marrying *me*. He's not exactly on this planet among us, anyway." She smiled at Jakub sweetly.

"Is this a joke?"

"Only one person in that group over there even lives here in San Antonio. Does it *look* like a joke? Besides, you and me in front of a priest would *never* be a joke. This was actually my idea."

As they moved closer to the crowd he began to recognize the assorted entourage. Willie was there with Carl and the kids, Sarah stood with an older middle-aged woman that looked to perhaps be in her 50s. He was surprised to see that Sedric had not made himself scarce, either, along with Darcy and Jeanette.

"She's a relative," Lindsey said, "She's a parishioner here, so that's why you get to do this. She likes weddings. She also went after the elderly priest because he can get through the ceremony, but he won't be asking any questions."

The Rose Window. That's where they were. She had said it was her favorite place in all of the Missions. It had a legacy that was somewhat not factual, but it's the thought that counts.

The story went that a Spanish sculptor was entrusted to create this ornate window in the late 1700s, and in the commission he snuck a fast one. He had personally dedicated this window to the love of his life, Rosa, and once it was complete and delivered, he sent word for his wife to come from Spain and join him in Texas.

In a heart-wrenching tragedy, his beloved Rosa was lost at sea while sailing to America. The legend grew, and the window itself, with its ornate features became a legacy of love, no matter what the actual facts of the matter might have been. It looked almost out of place, crumbling stone around it with a window barely four feet off of the ground.

It was that story of love that captivated the imagination and heart of a young Veronica.

The sun was shining and the temperature was warm, but he felt the chill up his spine and the short hairs rising on the back of his neck.

He was not alone.

Apparently not all of the wedding spectators were going to be human, and what had seemed silly to Jakub only 60 seconds ago now seemed like the most natural and necessary thing on Earth. He let Lindsey guide him up to the Window, up to an elderly clergyman who gave him a gentle smile while peering at him over his glasses.

"You must be the groom..." he stated absentmindedly, holding his head back as he attempted to adjust his eyes to the written notes he had hidden from view in the pages of a Bible that he held in a quivering hand. He glanced over Jakub's shoulder and called, "May I have the wedding party?"

As Jakub stood there, the world seemed to turn sideways, as if everything had shifted on its axis, and he had not even realized that Aiden was standing slightly behind him in a very nice suit Jakub knew he didn't own.

"What are *you* doing here?" Jakub whispered.

"I'm your best man, knucklehead!" he whispered back with a hiss through grinning teeth, covertly brandishing a pair of rings, "Now shut up and roll with it. Girl *traded the farm* for you."

It wasn't registering. He was beginning to feel like he'd walked into a dream again. Jakub had no recollection of anything that had been said by the old man as he looked at the profile next to him, felt the paralysis when he looked into her eyes like a sailor overboard on the North Sea. It was all so perfectly wrong.

Aiden nudged him, placed something in his hand.

Rings.

Thin, old, gold. That was when with the last bit of strength he had, he let go.

Her hands were shaking, thin, soft like the gentlest touch of lambskin, and as he slid the rings on he knew he was lost somewhere so large, so far away that he would never see the home he knew ever again.

Jakub didn't care. The blushing on her face as he spoke, the scent of lavender that flowed in a place that didn't seem to belong, sunshine on the back of his neck, warm like the face of God. He could have died and it might have been a moment of perfection. As he sank into her eyes again, he almost held his breath. What Lindsey slid onto his finger was the largest diamond he'd ever seen in his life, encased in rows of purple amethysts set in a jet black setting.

He was a man on fire, slowly burning from the inside out, building with intensity every second that passed on a surreal plateau and only they seemed to be on top of it. He'd heard the words "I do" escape her lips, but the way the words sank to his ears felt anything but surrogate.

"*You may kiss the bride...*"

It wasn't so much spoken as something that flowed into him, and she folded into him first.

They say that when seahorses mate, they entwine into a dance in the morning, and the male, being the one who bears the young, receives the injection that impregnates him from the female. She bestows something onto him that is possessive, all-encompassing, and he is then attached to everything that issues forth from that point on.

It was a moment that could have been frozen for eternity, and Jakub would have ridden that wave like a top ranked international surfer.

Her lips were cold and yet pristine, and he'd forgotten that there were other people present. It was the eruption of applause, and the sudden realization that he would have to cower back into the realm of real life that brought a broken heart from the moment.

It was possible that he might never see a moment like this again while he drew breath. At least not if Sarah could help it. She was fit to be tied.

This was going to be something Sarah wouldn't let go of for some time, if ever. It was obvious that she looked as if she'd been burned.

Aiden stayed close on Jakub.

"I think I just kissed the most beautiful girl still on Earth."

"I think the most beautiful girl still on Earth might've kissed *you*. At least that was how it looked from where I was standing. And I think some really heavy decisions are being made right now as we speak. Don't be surprised if she shows up on your doorstep one day. And I'll tell ya right now, you're an absolute fucking idiot if you don't ask her in first. That girl's all about you, I don't care what she might've said. My gut tells me that she set a trap, you fell into it, and my advice is to let her catch ya."

"You know when you start getting drunk, or you hit the pipe and that feeling comes in, you're not screwed up yet, you can function, but you look at the world and it all just seems *right*?"

"Yeah."

Jakub smiled blissfully and said, "I feel like that."

Maria knew that Jakub was curious about her, but he seemed to honestly have no indication that he knew who she was. For now, that was probably best. She could see in the way that he behaved that he was a gentle, decent type. It wasn't hard to understand what Veronica saw in him. In some ways, he reminded her of Al.

In some sense of it, she could see the shine in his eyes that were from someone deeply in love, but the sadness was there. He carried it with him everywhere that he went. She had seen him for who he actually was, and she had seen her daughter, buried but very much alive somewhere. She had heard about Veronica's love for him from her own mouth in a way that was so much better kept as a secret.

How it had happened seemed still to be surreal, but it was undeniable, and unmistakable.

At this point, Maria had lost all of her children, yet still managed to gain a son. There would be time to develop that relationship, but that time wasn't now. So many things for him to work out, very likely in the same process she had done herself and soon it would be time for her to step in and make herself available.

She had noticed several other things as they had dinner, though. For some reason, Jakub's sister Willow had an extreme aversion to that girl Sarah. It bordered on immediate outright hatred. Didn't know what the story was, but there was definitely no love lost. At one point it made things somewhat uncomfortable. Maria had to admit that she didn't have much use for the girl, either. Especially with what she'd seen her put Lindsey through in the past.

"Welcome to Texas," Willow said to her, "but be aware that this is a place where justice just seems to... *happen*." No one else really appeared to know or understand what the actual topic of that discussion was, but the girl Sarah seemed to know exactly what it was about, and she had paled. The daggers in Willow's eyes would have made anyone take a step back.

It would have been an uneven matchup. Sarah looked like she belonged at a debutante ball, and Willow looked like she could take anyone in a back alley. But Willow had been as sweet as sugar to Maria, and even called her "Mama" and kept checking on her to make sure everything was okay.

Lindsey? She was going to be okay. Anyone with half of a brain saw what had happened today, and Maria held no ill feelings whatsoever with it. For Maria's part, she'd went along with this knowing that everyone just needed to heal. It also didn't hurt that she gained a brand new and concrete perspective herself on exactly what was going to happen when she finally died.

Knowing these things was certainly half of the battle.

She could have gone out and found another mate herself, but something in her just never wanted to let go enough. It didn't make her better or worse, and maybe if someday down the road Jakub decided he might need to try his hand at love a little closer to home, she would have no problem whatsoever with it. She might even nudge him out of the nest a bit. Unlike her, he was still young. He still had time.

She wasn't in a place to say anything, but Maria really hoped he would eventually use it wisely before it all went away. There are some things that should never be left undone.

enjoy your problems

Sure, it sounded crazy. Almost stupid. But she had managed to pull off a wedding without a hitch, fully surprising the groom, who thankfully didn't find it silly, and that alone is a major feat for anyone. Especially doing a lot of it completely under the radar.

Sarah had, as usual, been about as useful as a football bat, but why add her to this equation, anyway? She was doing it for a lost friend, and the guy who finally got her.

It made for a damned fine excuse, anyway.

For better or worse. Lindsey herself had not ever been able to have those real conversations. She fought the voice off in her head that knew the truth and screamed it. Feeling like she was defending herself and other things that really didn't deserve to be defended, they needed to be brought out into the open, out into the light, but doing it was a damned near impossibility. She did all of this wedding hoopla for her friend, yes. At least that was how it appeared on its surface. Appearances could be dealt with. Half of surviving life was the art of the impression. People deal better with their impressions of things than what the facts actually are.

She *did* love her friend. But this was the closest she was now ever going to get to those old Hollywood dreams she'd had before Sarah, when all she'd wanted was to be on the beach walking down the aisle in a sunset wedding with Jakub.

Lindsey had loved Jakub first. It was a pull that couldn't be explained, couldn't be defined, and she dared to not let it ever come out of her mouth because the ridicule and torment if she had guessed wrong would have been more than she could have possibly borne.

Grand-mère Papillon had pulled the wedding rings from her own finger after her grandfather had died, cuddled a teenaged Lindsey close to her and said, "These are yours, mon chéri, may they bring you all of the love and wholeness that they have brought me, and may they bring you the one who is worthy to put them on your finger." She remembered the softness of her hands, skin crepe-paper thin, the soft eyes and smile as if everything holy had just been placed into her. Grand-mère died three days later.

There was right plenty Sarah didn't know about her. Didn't really care to find out, either.

But those were the very rings she'd had Jakub place on her fingers to "fool" the officiant. And she just couldn't bring herself to take them off.

In fact, she might just not.

The thing she couldn't get out of her head was what Willie had said at dinner after the ceremony. They had bumped into each other near the restrooms, and Willie had a look on her face that held an intense expression that was a puzzle Lindsey couldn't solve. She had something she was about to say, and it was clear she would not be deterred from saying it.

"Walk with me," Willie commanded with all of the authority of a five-star general, slipping through the exit door. Lindsey followed, out into the sunshine. She fished a cigarette from her purse and lit it, taking a deep drag as she seemed to think.

"I'm only going to say this once. And I am going to deny it if I have to, you know, have a *really* sketchy memory. You've done an incredible thing here, but we're beyond bullshittin' and you need to hear this."

"Okay..." Lindsey said, feeling both nervous and confused. She really didn't like confrontations.

"That man in there, *my brother*, has been mad as a hatter, shitstorm crazy over you for years, through the last four serious relationships he's had. He dates them, fucks them, settles for them, but he only talks about *you*. Until this VR thing with

Veronica. He's always been bent out of shape that you wouldn't even give 'im the time of day. And then all this," she said, waving her hand in a circle. Her gaze was softening.

"I think you missed something." Willie said pointedly, "I think you're afraid of something. I don't know what it is, and I ain't gonna ask. But you have the face of an angel, and a disposition to match, you ain't stuck on yourself, and I get it. I know what he sees in you, and don't you think for a goddamned second that it's completely went away."

Lindsey felt like a bucket of ice had been dumped on her. But Willie wasn't finished.

She noticed that a girl was eavesdropping on their conversation, leaning up against the bumper of a car about 25 feet away with an Emory board, filing down the fingernails on her left hand, chewing gum. She made a little pop that was almost inaudible. Lindsey noticed the tattoos on her right hand, the lotus flower peeking under the sleeve onto her wrist. The girl had a copper colored buzz cut with hoop earrings, wide starlet sunglasses pushed up on top of her head. She casually gave a side glance at the pair.

"Look, you have no idea what a perfect match you are for him. I ain't trying to bust up what you've got going on, well, okay, yeah I am, but honestly it'd hurt you more than it would me if ya sacked her ass. Cuz if all this," she made another swirl with the cigarette, "Ever goes away, you have that boy's heart in checkmate position. You're a queen that has a king locked in tight, and he ain't goin' far. I suggest you use that advantage and take what's yours. Because it was yours *first*."

The shaved girl looked up through incredible ice blue eyes that seemed almost inhuman, pointing the emery board at Lindsey with a couple of light jabs and nodded. She gave a smile and a wink, popped another bubble.

"I honestly don't think I ever knew that," Lindsey said breathlessly.

"Bullshit. You suspected it. I tried to tell ya that at the diner. I think deep down you knew, you just had doubts. You doubted *yourself*. And you gotta do something about that. You don't see yourself the way the rest of the world sees you, and that's to ya own detriment, sistah. We should sneak back inside before they miss us. So I'm gonna 'forget', and you ain't. Okay?"

"Okay."

The shaved girl was gone. Lindsey realized that she had been looking at the hoodie girl from the Dallas Airport.

There was something about that girl that just felt right, like she was meant to find her, but she had no idea where to look. And it wasn't anything like a relationship or a sisterhood, it was deeper, and closer to home. Like, if she could find that girl, she would find herself.

She had kissed Jakub again on the cheek before she left. It was something she'd always wanted to do, but had forced restraint on herself. Perhaps restraint was something she needed to start learning to let go of more. She'd felt him blissfully breathe her in, even in that moment with eyes closed and content, like she were a breeze from heaven and it broke her. Sarah had gone wild-eyed with jealously but said nothing. She hadn't regained control over the fact Lindsey had kissed Jakub on the lips at the ceremony.

Sarah could fuck herself.

After what Willie had said to Sarah earlier, it was plain there was bad blood, and now Lindsey understood why. But there was nothing could be done about that just yet. What was done was done. Lindsey was interested in what Willie had meant by "justice", and from the conversation they had outside the restaurant, she knew that it wasn't the relationship Willie was angry about.

It was the context in which it had started, the lies and the abuse.

Sarah had an expiration date. That wasn't even a question.

She felt like she had just gained another sister that was probably meaner and more aggressive than Veronica ever was. Not that it made her miss

Veronica any less. All things appear to come in their time.

Willie had pulled her aside again before they left and said, "Don't be a stranger. If I don't hear from you in two weeks, I'm calling *you*. As far as I'm concerned, you're family. I'm gonna treat you as such." She smiled again and pointed a finger saying, "I'm serious. Call me."

Now she was looking down at the rings on her left hand, and they felt like they belonged there. Something was missing, besides the obvious. She had time to put that together. It felt as real to her as her arm. Lindsey was officially checked out of this Sarah deal, but she was gonna have to play the game until everything else came together.

She knew she was supposed to call out for someone, a name that was familiar, that she *knew*. It couldn't make its way to the tip of her tongue, but was exotic, refined, like the bloodline Lindsey herself descended from.

She forced her mind to run on all cylinders as if it were an Enigma Machine. She wanted to crack the code she'd placed before it, the name that girl had said to her in the dream back in the airport at San Antonio, and pull out the word from the game of charades Rector had at the convention. It was familiar, something she interacted with every day, but the connection stayed just out of gripping distance.

Chairs. Something to do with chairs.

Lindsey took a deep breath and removed herself from everything around her as the name floated in quietly and gently, landing on her mind like a feather that had been trapped in a faraway breeze.

Corisande.

I own a chair from the Corisande Collection.

The new sight had opened another layer to the world that Darcy had imagined, had heard about, but had never actually seen herself.

She had noticed the two girls off to the side, watching the ceremony and acting as if it was the most normal thing in the world. The taller one with the long, wavy hair was the girl she'd seen at the Tinder Statesman, the one that had given her sight back. The other was wearing a white dress. The scene would have been strange if Darcy had not seen the video before. That was obviously Veronica.

The most interesting part of the spectacle was during the actual wedding ceremony when Veronica walked up to the blonde girl at the beginning of the vows and seemed to transfigure into her. Darcy knew she was the only one that saw that.

Whatever the connection was between them, it had appeared to be very good.

She was every bit as pretty as advertised, and Darcy had been the only one to see them specifically, it appeared. The girl from the

Statesman recognized that Darcy had spotted her and flashed that signature smile with a wave. She seemed very excited.

Veronica, on the other hand seemed both very happy and also as if she'd lost something at the same time. She was holding a bouquet of lavender that no one else was able to see, but the intense scent had been very detectable to anyone that was there at the time.

It seemed to be a thing with those two, always the lavender scent. And they both looked so similar, like they were related or something. The eyes. They both had the same eyes.

There was something about seeing all of these other people involved in the lives of the living there. It was as if everyone had their own entourage working in the background trying to make sure everything was at least going on in a tolerable way. She heard a couple of them talking business in the days since her eyes had been opened by the girl, and there was still a knowledge and expectation of secrecy in everything.

Even their discussions were hushed when it came to direct conversations about the people they represented. It was plain to see that for the most part, they all took it very seriously. On the other hand, they behaved like any other group of people would, with some having cliques, and many of them giving grief to each other and playing around like you'd hear in any business office in the country.

It didn't escape her that Clayton was nowhere to be seen, and to be honest, Darcy liked it better that way for the moment.

The girl made a beeline for Darcy and with a warm smile said, "I see you have no hangers-on today. That's just as well. I have requested new arrangements for different accompaniment on your behalf. I think it will be much more beneficial. But watch out for Stanton. I fear he may be a little bit unhinged. Not that he wasn't in the first place. For the record, I opposed his appointment when it was suggested, so that wasn't my fault. It was just left for me to solve it."

The girl looked around with a sly smile. "You see the best man over there?" She asked, pointing over to a young man near Jakub. "I think he might be the kind of guy you're looking for. Could be the time to let out that little cougar you've been hiding in there. Don't worry, he's not *that* much younger than you. You should say hello to him. Don't let that one get away. He's very single."

She felt giddy, and the girl prodded her again, "Go ahead. Introduce yourself. It's not like he and Jakub haven't been talking about you or anything."

"Oh no," Darcy said, horrified, "What did they say?"

"Oh, I don't know," the girl purred, "Something about you being a complete hottie. Little things like that. How you'd be the perfect girl for him to meet. He's *very* interested. He's even wondering what you look like. I already know he's going to be very pleasantly surprised."

"How do you know that?"

"Remember I told you about a gift you are getting? Well, dearie, that young stud right there is it. Now quit talking to me, and go talk to him. It's not like he hasn't been waiting for ya. His name is Aiden. Ay-den. This is easy. You got this."

Then the girl vanished into the wind.

She began walking, plodding, almost. It was one of those times when you're walking one foot after the other and you feel like you're walking the surface of the moon. Like everything else has disconnected, and you're uncontrollably on autopilot. As she reached him, Aiden turned and locked eyes with her. She wasn't sure if she was under a spotlight or a tractor beam.

"Hi! I'm Aiden. I'm one of the other buccaneers on this pirate ship here. It's good to meet you," he said, with a television star grin that seemed to fill her up like a kite in the wind. She could feel the warm energy on him, almost like a radiating floor heater.

"Darcy. Darcy Kitchens." *I slurred. Dammit, I bet I slurred.*

"Ah. *You're* Darcy. I've heard a lot about you. All good, of course. Then it's double a pleasure to meet you. Are you coming to dinner with us? I'm pretty sure you're invited. If not, you are now."

Now he felt electric. The heat from him seemed to vibrate now and tingle.

"Yes, I'd love to," she heard herself respond.

"That's wonderful!" Although she could hear the confidence in his voice, and feel the vibrations from him, she also could detect the panic, the fear that he did *not* want to screw this up. She decided to take the upper hand. The girl was right. If she was physical, she'd kiss her right about now.

"You know," Darcy said with the most seductive smile that she could come up with, hoping it wasn't too much, "When we get over there, I'd like to take a little time, y'know, so we can get to know each other a little better." She saw his face light up.

Touch him. You gotta touch him! Now!

"I'll see you there?" She asked, stoking his forearm.

He stopped to breathe, "I wouldn't miss it."

She casually turned and strolled back to her car, leaving him there.

Don't turn around. Don't...

She stole a glance just in time to see him stifling a cheer. Darcy couldn't have stopped the smile that was spreading over her face with a thousand horses. When she finally reached her car, she got into the driver's seat, shut the door, and had a good old-fashioned, high decibel *squee*.

This one's mine. I totally own this guy.

no wasted moments

This had been a day for the history books. Jakub wasn't sure of a time when so many completely different things had happened in a single day. He was trying to chew over what he had witnessed and been a part of.

He put a ring on Lindsey Barber's finger. She had put a *really* beautiful one on his. Those two sentences were previously not on his radar of even being a remote possibility, in any circumstance or situation. They were two sentences that had seemed to only be destined for orbit, not connection.

Too bad I didn't get to consummate that one, Jakub thought, and immediately felt guilty. He knew that wasn't the point of the whole thing, it had been done in honor of Veronica. It was really an astounding gesture, but he was sure none of them realized where he'd been about Lindsey. In fact, Lindsey probably still didn't get that he'd been eyeing her for years. But at least now he knew without a shadow of a doubt that she didn't hate him, and that she actually never had. That was certainly worth the price of admission in any event.

Jakub kept bouncing back and forth, like the thoughts wouldn't come to any solid conclusion that he could say was fact on its face. No matter what direction he went, he felt guilty about something. He felt guilty about not acting, not saying the right things when he had the chance, and guilt all over again because he was crazy about both of them. Even more guilt that both of them felt like a subtext to these new things that were happening to him.

The last year had been a complete mind job.

He went from miserable and drunk, to having one of the most beautiful women to walk the Earth madly in love with him, and the other seeming like she might just possibly follow suit. He could now see and talk to dead people. That was pretty wild, too. Every session with Darcy led to something new he hadn't known before, his dreams bringing him in contact with real people that had passed before him, living in a world that he was only beginning to scratch the surface of.

Aiden had seemed to have no particular opinion of things, he just listened and didn't act like anything Jakub had said to him was anything out of the ordinary. Okay, so that wasn't exactly the truth. He was pretty much an active cheerleader in all of this, and was still running amok with a lot more left to teach as he went on his various ventures. He had become more than some guy Jakub just met one day in a burger shack. He was a real, true friend. One of the few friends Jakub had ever had in his life. This was an improvement.

Sure, Aiden moved around a lot, but Jakub knew that no matter what, he would always have a place for him to crash, a place that was safe with at least one person that cared about his well-being. Jakub noticed that Aiden didn't really talk about his family much, and also didn't seem to visit them or call them too often, which led him to believe that maybe there was something going on there that he would eventually crack and talk about. It was better not to push on these things, because eventually he'd come out with them. It was just the nature of the beast.

Willie, as usual, had her little brother's back. Whatever that was at dinner, she knew something that he didn't, and she wanted to do some creative rearrangement to Sarah's face. It seemed that she'd known about what she was doing before he had. Problem was, she used the word *justice*, and when Willie says that, you might want to sleep with an eye open and a shotgun handy. He laughed out loud. He couldn't help it. Willie is just a girl you don't wanna fuck with. She'd mellowed over the years, but that streak was still in there, and it would be unwise to cross it.

He looked at the ring again, solid black metal, black gold from what he understood, amethyst bars on the sides bolstering a large diamond. He had been told that it was a Herkimer diamond, and both

Lindsey and Darcy had explained that the amethysts were actually from a pair of earrings Veronica wore every day, so her energy was attached to it. The diamond Lindsey had put a lot of time and energy into locating. Both of them were bound together into something that for him had turned his world completely upside down and put him in a place where everything he'd ever known was up to be examined and questioned.

It was a very good new world to be in and be a part of. He felt like he might just now have the best team behind him, and still had no clue what was coming next, but it made his heart feel good. At the end of the day, no one could argue with that being a great position.

Lindsey didn't hate him. She had never hated him. And he finally got to see what he'd always wanted to see in her eyes.

Himself.

Now he could focus more on Veronica and where the rest of this adventure was going to take him.

He felt like he was dancing on a razor's edge, and there were flames below him. He thought about what Hester had said, and wondered what Shelaine might have to say. They did say he could call for them anytime, even if they usually showed up in his dreams.

He decided to take a moment and see what happened. "Shelaine? Are you there? I need to talk."

Jakub couldn't see her, but he heard her respond. "Right here, Chief."

"So I can't see you, but I can hear you."

"Yeah, you're clairaudient. It's a little lower frequency to tap into. Takes less energy to connect over. What's up? How can I help?"

"Woman troubles. Or maybe woman *confusion* would be more accurate."

"I figured this would come up, and I can give you a good answer before you ask the question. You're allowed to love them both as fiercely and passionately as you want to. I know it's a hard one to figure out from your position. I know you think it's a thing of loyalty, and I know you think one loves you and the other one doesn't, or that you're supposed to love one more than the other. Look at your hand. Think about it this way, you're widowed from one, and the other was supposed to happen first anyway."

"How do you figure 'happened first'? She didn't have anything to say to me before Veronica."

Shelaine responded, "What girl is going to hunt your sister, fly out to Texas, arrange all of this for a friend, stand in a wedding ceremony with you and have you put rings on her and not like you more than a little bit? Women don't do things just to be friendly. There is always a reason we don't say, and usually an ulterior motive. And I'd like to note for the record, none of that is fake to her. She's still wearing those rings, and she will still be wearing them the next time you lay eyes on her. Yeah, you did in fact have a ceremony with two girls at once. But right now, you're in a place where neither of them functionally matter at the end of the day. Walk your road. It's time. We got you on this. Be glad that both of them love you with every fiber of their beings, because it's gonna become critical down the road. Get over this either-or barrier, because you, Sir, are in a quite unique position. A lot of people have put in a great deal of hard work for you, and it's just beginning. The wooly's coming. Enjoy these weeks, because it'll be a while before you get this kind of rest again. Love's gonna be the first thing on your mind, I get that. But it's also gonna be the last thing on your mind, because you'll need to focus on what you're doing."

Jakub took a deep breath. "I'm nervous as hell. I might even say that I'm scared."

"Scared is not a crime. Battle is scary. War is scary. The Middle Zone is scary. Tonight, you're safe. Enjoy it without any kind of regret or apprehension. Go with it. If it will help, eventually I'll connect you with Cori again. You're going to be talking to her before this is all over."

"The girl with the butterfly on her leg?"

"That would be the one."

"Who is she in charge of?"

"Really? Do the math, son!"

"I know that The Lady was in charge of Veronica, and I know Stanton was Darcy's advocate, so that means..."

"Look at your hand."

"Cori is Lindsey's advocate."

"Uh, yeah. Starting to get it now?"

"But I remember what she said. I know I wasn't supposed to, but I do anyway. So I'm not in some weird delusion about Lindsey?"

Shelaine laughed. "You just kissed the girl in a wedding ceremony. That wasn't no little 'let's fake it' peck. We were *there*. We saw it. What you did today was a real thing. I don't know if that was a kiss I watched, or a tonsil cleaning." Jakub could almost feel Shelaine shaking her head before she finished, "Sometimes you two are so damned slow."

The young clerk took the folder in her hand from her friend that was standing at the counter.

"Would you be a sweetie and do me a favor? I didn't get to file this, and now I hafta go pick up the kids, and if I don't get out of here, I'll be late. You know how this is. I start gettin' calls and letters and weepin' and wailin' if I ain't there on time. Everything's ready to go, just enter it in the system, plop it where it goes, easy-peasey."

"Sure, I can get that for ya."

She thumped the folder open. Everything appeared to be in place. Marriage license signed by the officiant, everything good. The label on the corner was printed out correctly, large letters RISER-BARBER along with the filing codes. Entering the information into the system, she slapped it all together for the night's filing.

As she finished up for the day and got in her car to relax, there was a piece of important information she had not been presented with, and would never know.

300 miles to the south, a slightly modified copy of those documents existed, with a few differing minor details. The documents she'd filed were legally binding, and both parties were utterly oblivious to the fact that she had them in her possession. The copy to the south held the name of a dead girl.

And that copy was not technically legal. But the Church seemed to like that one a lot.

What folks don't know might not hurt 'em.

stars that shine for you

His little cottage, if you could call it that, was rather spartan, as if it were a secret hideout from which he prepared to do greater things. A man in his 30s with light brown surfer-shock hair and about two days stubble was stretched out on a sofa in the living room with the baby blue of a UCLA shirt and a Southwestern style blanket over him.

"That's Aiden," the Lady said, "He's been here a lot more recently. We kinda set that up so your boy has a decent role model around him. There are plans for him, too. He doesn't know what they are yet, of course, but alas, Baby Girl, that's one of the downsides of this job. You know more than you're supposed to, and only so much you can technically or legally do about it."

"What's that?" Veronica said, motioning over to the aquarium.

"You."

"How do you figure that?" She asked.

"It was a gift from another one of his friends. He named her Angelica Luz. Ring any bells?"

It was the name she'd picked out if she had ever had a daughter. So he remembered. And now her daughter was a fish.

"Take a good look at it. I think it's a very impressive creature, myself. Look at the fin on the bottom. If you're here at the right time, you'll hear him gush about it. He loves that fish. Always talks about you at some point. It's easy to love the things you can relate in your head, I guess." Her companion gestured at the tank. The fish had a singular fin that waved back and forth to propel it. The fish immediately came to the side of the tank as if to be petted like a dog.

"There are apparently a few attributes that he and the guy that gave it to him relate to you. Bunch of stuff about darkness, electricity, and being a homebody."

"Thanks."

"I aim to please. Anyway, we're here to peek in on our boy, right?"

"My husband. We're here so I can see my husband."

Aiden shifted from where he was sleeping on the couch and pulled his covers tighter over him to get more warmth. "Fucking air conditioning," he murmured, still asleep.

"I got him a little girlfriend," her companion said, the trademark grin of hers on her face, "He doesn't know it yet, but I hooked him up real good. Everybody seems to agree that it's a good thing."

"Everybody?"

"Yeah. Everybody. Stanton took a little more convincing, though. Okay, so he didn't actually agree, but screw that guy. I swear that bastard argues with about anything I come up with. He's a petulant little brat."

"Stanton?"

"Nevermind. Doesn't really concern you and what you're doing. Yet, anyway. Fits into my plan really well, though!" She flashed a big toothy grin and moved towards another door with a single metal sign that read STARS PARKING. Her companion thumped the sign with a finger and an audible ping. "Boys will be boys. I would've thought, at his age..."

"He *really* likes the Stars," Veronica said.

"Your *husband*. Now, anyway. I mean, as far as that goes. But our boy's through this door."

Her companion seemed to melt through the door, and Veronica followed her, the soft moonlight reflecting into the room and turning it into a grayish violet landscape. "Oh, baby, this is *mine!*" The companion said excitedly as she turned and plopped into a papasan chair in the corner. She kicked her feet up on top of the bed with a smile.

He lay on his bed, stretched out on one side, deeply under. She wished that she knew how to get into his head, sink into his dreams, to connect with him like they used to do. It was good to be out of the VR headset, because now there was a whole world out there, wrapped and woven into the one that the incarnate were in. Jakub had no idea she was here in the room with him, watching him, admiring him.

But Veronica knew that she would learn all of this and more. It would happen, even if it wasn't today.

Luna lay on the pillow next to him, the pillow that in another life would have been hers. She stretched out on the bed next to him, knowing that he wouldn't detect her presence, part of that fact hurting her deeply, but also grateful that she could now do even that. She was reaching to put an arm around him, but it simply didn't stop. There was no resistance between her form and his.

"Easy there, Girlie," her companion said. "You don't wanna get too close to him like that. You could cause him physical problems, like hurt him and stuff. I know you wanna learn how to get into his dreams. That'll happen soon enough. Remember, this is a process, you have to learn the basics and work through things to get better at 'em."

She knew that all she could do was watch him sleep. If she waited long enough, she could watch him get up, shower, go to work, all the menial things that are so taken for granted until they all go away and you're left watching everything like it's through a window.

"Who's this?" Veronica heard from the corner. She was pointing at a framed, autographed picture that was hanging on the wall. Leaning in, she read the name on the bottom, "Mike Mo-dan-o. Hmph. Never heard of him."

"Mo-dah-no."

"Whatever."

"Whatever? Guy has a Stanley Cup. He's in the Hall of Fame! Least you could do is say his name right. Besides, Jakub loses his shit if you pronounce it wrong." Veronica was surprised at how fast it had riled her up. Hell, she wasn't even connected to any of that.

"Who's losing their shit now? I didn't know you were a hockey girl..."

"I'm not. I'm a Jakub girl, and hockey comes with it."

"Aight. I can deal with that. Notice how they keep getting cold? That's because of us. We take up some of the ambient energy so we can even be here. That slows the remaining atomic structures down, which in turn makes the temperature drop. I figured you'd like that, since you're into all that geeky kinda stuff."

"How do you even know the word 'geeky'?"

"I hang out with all you cool kids."

"Isn't 'groovy' more your thing?"

"Chica! Now you're going out of bounds. That was Mama's time, not mine."

She tried to focus on Jakub, who was actually next to her in real life and real time, not that she actually had a connection to either anymore. Watching his chest rise and fall with each breath still made her feel like she was home.

"Have you seen his paperwork yet?" Her companion asked.

"No. I've been with you, remember?"

"Yes, I just didn't know if it'd come up in Review."

"No."

"You've sorta complicated things with that electronic technology stunt. You little scientist, you."

"Hey, that wasn't intentional!"

"True, but I think you complicated things in a good way, and I know that doesn't make sense, but it will." The look on her face was like a mother adoring a toddler. "You know there's a lot of history in this little clique."

"What little clique? Do you mean the soldiers? I already met them. We had that chat."

"Well, we can talk about all of that later. Bottom line is that I've been your advocate most of your life. I was your advocate with this whole electronic merry-go-round stuff, so *that* raised an eyebrow or two. Why am I telling you all of this again? But I think everything will go quite well, everything considered, from here on out. Would you like to commence your honeymoon? I guess that's the question."

"Whaddya mean?"

"Well, I know what I said before about your skill level, but I have this little trick in my back pocket. You're gonna lay right there, and I'm gonna push you over into his dreams, and you guys can do whatever it is you wanna do until he wakes up." She winked and giggled.

"What happens when he wakes up?"

"You're just gonna pop back out. Nothing to worry about. I can't do this all the time, takes a lot of energy for me, but I think this is earned in your case. Where do you wanna go?"

She felt herself grin widely. *One place I've always wanted to go.*

Her companion stood up and walked over to Jakub. She closed her eyes and briskly rubbed her hands together, then placed one hand on his forehead. He squirmed and shifted positions as if he were uncomfortable. Veronica felt a hand on her forehead, and then a sensation as if she were melting.

Veronica opened her eyes to brilliant sunshine and perfect baby blue skies. The water spread out in front of her like a blanket of pristine sea glass, the salty breeze gently floating in with a caress. She felt the wooden deck of the bungalow under her bare foot.

Oh yeah, baby. This is more like it.

Jakub was next to her on a white canvas reclining chair in a thin robe, eyes gently closed as if he were taking it all in and relaxing. She could tell that he had nothing on under the robe. It was standing up where it normally wouldn't.

She felt the giddiness in her breast as he opened his eyes. He reached out his hand to her as he looked into her eyes. She grabbed it, felt his skin in her hand.

"Where is this place? I mean, where *are* we?" He asked, a smile of contentment on his face.

"Bora Bora," Veronica said with a satisfied sigh. "It *is* our honeymoon, after all."

thanks

I was eight. I wanted to read. Read something *real*. The encyclopedias were getting old, and I wanted something far away, away from the Bobbsey Twins, the Hardy Boys, and Nancy Drew. Those were my mother's books.

They were enjoyable, but dang it, I wanted something different. And then, a ray of light on the horizon, for my mother had committed a most egregious tactical error.

She started a public library.

Amongst those first tomes was some guy that had written a lot of books. And I mean, *a lot*. At least to an eight-year-old. And the staff was stupid. I've told you this before. Somewhat at length.

I read *Jaws*. I read *The Exorcist*. I read *The Shining*. I was picking up the wrong damned books. After questions such as the following:[1]

♦ What exactly are they doing in the shower that requires him to put his hand in the crack of her butt?

---

[1] Yes, these were the literal, verbatim questions I asked my mother.

- ♦ Why does the demon need a translator? He seemed to cuss perfectly fine to me.
- ♦ Does all work and no play *really* make Jack a dull boy? Why can't he just be good at typing?

My mother brought my checking out of books to a screeching halt without supervision.

Which is exactly like a fox walking up to a hen house and saying, "I don't want any chickens, ya hear? I just need three of those things over there with feathers on 'em."

To which the guard dog would reply, "Oh, well since you put it *that* way..."

So I met the books of Judy Blume, and girl questions started happening, which were redirected to the library.

"Don't ask me, go find a book about it."

Challenge accepted.

I was barred from *The Joy of Sex* and anything from Dr. Ruth Westheimer.

But then, I met a crook. And once I began reading the Bernie Rhodenbarr series of books, I knew that one day I wanted to write books, too. Asking my mother about autoerotic asphyxiation almost put her in the looney bin. I was about nine years old. I don't know which was worse, that she didn't know about it, or that I could describe it in such authoritative detail.

My library card was finally burned.

I owe a lot to Lawrence Block (I'd call you Larry, but this is like a permanent printing, you see). I owe much to Judy Blume, because with the advent of the Internet, they were two of the first writers that interacted with me, and I never forgot it. I was much older then, out of the military, and it still seemed like the gods were speaking happily and gently from Mount Olympus.

That's where I got my start.

It was Kurt Vonnegut that helped remove my filter. So for all those mothers who have young children that steal this book, read it, then come back with embarrassing questions... Sorry about that. But they should turn out okay and unscathed. I've now been on both sides of this.

But all of this is still Bernie's fault. He was just too interesting for me to ignore.

about the author

Sion Jones is a Welsh American ontologist and writer of magical realism.

His first published works were of poetry in 1992, and over the next decade, extended to three full-length poetry books and a novella. He began the Jakub Riser series in 2018, and is also the author of the Veil series.

Sion is a member of the Society of Professional Journalists and studied Journalism at Michigan State University.

He is currently published by Aethem Press in Austin, Texas.